ABOUT THIS BOOK

Welcome to the darker, sexier side of Havenwood Falls that many residents never speak of publicly, but most likely enjoy in secret. Venture into the SIN MC, the VIP rooms of Silk nightclub, and behind other closed doors, where you'll discover passion, unusual penchants, and just how far some will go for love. Hold on to your panties, because it's time to ride.

What do you do when Death's hot on your heels for messing with the afterlife order?

Yeah, I'm a smooth guy, generally. But some damned souls escaped the Infernum during my last visit, and now I'm Death's chew toy. I've gotta track and return these supernatural fugitives before they cause more carnage. Easy, right? Except Nyx, a vampire-demon hybrid, is leading these already corrupt souls astray and turning a secret town upside down during her pursuit for queendom of the Underworld. Crazy bitches come with crazy ideas.

I arrive in Havenwood Falls in the midst and madness of a Hot Cocoa and Cookie Crawl. I don't expect to be swallowed up by this mystical town with its own enchantments, luring me in with its hidden beauty. There are secrets much deeper than what appears on the surface. One in particular has sinful legs and silky hair I'm desperate to bury myself into. She's hooked me like a gullible puppy owner, trapped by those stunning eyes. I'm screwed. Literally.

Sadly, Death is still snapping at my ass, halting my attempts to unravel this beauty's darkest desires. The Infernum demands Nyx's soul be amongst the others to be returned, and I *will* reap them. I am their courier to Hell.

My name is Shade StormIron, and I am an Angel of Death.

HAVENWOOD FALLS SIN & SILK BOOKS

Taming the Beast by Nadirah Foxx

Plans Laid Bare by JD Nelson

Shift of Fate by Victoria Escobar

Stolen Wishes by Victoria Flynn

Damned Allure by Justine Winter

Savage Salvation by Kristie Cook

Dark Seduction by Michele G. Miller & R.K. Ryals

Soul Laid Bare by JD Nelson

Stray With Me by E.J. Fechenda

Chase the Flames by Desiree Lafawn

Flirting With Death by Nadirah Foxx

Also try the signature line, Havenwood Falls, the historical paranormal line, Legends of Havenwood Falls, and stories from the local supernatural college in Sun & Moon Academy.

Stay up to date at www.HavenwoodFalls.com

ALSO BY JUSTINE WINTER

DAMNED ALLURE

A HAVENWOOD FALLS SIN & SILK NOVELLA

JUSTINE WINTER

For your inner sass. Let her out.

CHAPTER 1

INFERNUM

"*F*uck me, you're a feisty one, aren't you? Don't you wanna play nice for Big Daddy?" I tease the bitch trying to wriggle free from my arm. She's a fighter, I'll give her that. I tighten my hold as we descend from the inky night sky, swirling like wisps of black smoke until we breach the realm boundaries to the Infernum.

"Take. Me. Back!" She huffs out every syllable, straining as she tries to halt my progress, using what strength and weight she has left to keep me from depositing her damned soul into Hell's special holding place. These buggers never think they'll be caught and end up here. It's fucking hilarious really—where else do they think their death will send them? Supernatural creatures are my worst clients, reckoning they can screw the world over and not be punished for it. Stupid bastards.

"Cut this shit out, or I'll make sure your time in the Infernum is as painful and torturous as possible."

She tuts. "You don't have that kind of power. You're just a messenger boy."

She laughs maniacally as though the fringe of the Infernum's entrance is already driving her crazy.

Screams and howls pierce the atmosphere; the walls bleed misery and torment, a promise of suffering for all trapped here. There's no escaping now.

I let her go, knowing her soul is now anchored to the Infernum's clutches.

"I may be Death's bitch," I begin, taking a cursory glance around the area. Fire and brimstone burst through cracks in this sweat box, and sulfur permeates the charred air. It's bloody offensive to my senses, like some inconsiderate arsehole's left a dead animal to rot in the scorching sun. The only thing missing here is the blowflies to gorge on these corpses. "But at least I don't have to spend an eternity listening to these acoustics and smelling shit all day. Have fun, bitch!"

I turn and walk away, releasing any hidden ties I still have on her. I meant it before—I'm not bound for an existence here. I'm an approved visitor only. These evil motherfucking souls are not bringing me down with them.

A loud whistle cuts through the oppressive air. "I see you're still making friends. You ever try bringing someone in without pissing them off, Shade?"

"What fun would that be?" I let a cheeky smile cover my face, though it's somewhat difficult to see when my face lacks flesh. Really, I'm just showing off a perfect set of teeth all denture-wearing oldies are jealous of. I'm still the sexiest skeleton around. I've got big bones, if you know what I mean. "Nobody ever wants to come down here willingly. You were the same, Sapphire. I almost broke a nail delivering you."

"You'd need nails first, Shade. Have you missed me?" The vampire sulks toward me, reaching out to touch my chest cavity.

"Babe, you might have been smokin' hot up top on Earth, but down here your skin looks like it's been ravished by moths. You're holier than all the angels." I roar with laughter, momentarily silencing the usual musical screams.

"At least I've still got skin." She pushes away from me, taking any more thoughts of seduction with her. Thank fuck. One more year down here and a human corpse will be fresher than this stubborn supernatural stiff. There's no talent for beauty contests down here.

"Sapphire, before you go, there's something you forgot," I call out, smirking to myself.

"You're not getting a kiss, Shade. Please yourself," she replies over her shoulder, not daring to look my way.

"Oh, I will, but really, you forgot something . . ." I wait until she gives in, striding with purpose to me. Her eyes widen as she catches sight of my bony hands holding something she wants back. I flex my fingers over the mass.

"What are you doing?" She seems horrified, which is quite impressive considering her home is the Infernum.

"I told you, you forgot something."

"I see that." She grits her teeth. "But what are you *doing* to it?"

"Chill, babe. I'm just squeezing a piece of your arse."

CHAPTER 2

DEATH

*F*ucking priceless.

"You finished torturing us poor souls yet?"

I stop when I hear the deep timbre of an old acquaintance. I lean against a sweat-dripping wall, crossing my skeletonized arms over my chest, my hooded black cloak flowing freely around me. I'm a handsome bastard, really.

"You ever had a woman fall apart in front of you, my friend?" I ask.

"We both know I don't do emotions, Shade." Jax, a long-serving Infernum inmate, speaks.

I shake my head. "I mean literally. That shit is hilarious." I laugh out loud all over again. The old vamp's face had been quite the picture of horror. Talk about embarrassing. "She put her arse right in my hands. Don't get more forward than that."

We giggle like a pair of schoolgirls.

"Man, this place fucks you up for good." Jax shakes his head, and I realize how tired the old bear shifter looks. Amazingly, he's endured the Infernum for a century already, and considering how slow time moves here, that's a feat in itself. Most souls crumble after five minutes because it seems like five *decades* have already passed.

"You coping? You're looking uglier these days," I quip, remembering the youthful shifter all those years ago.

"Speak for yourself, mate. Did you lose weight? You're looking gaunt."

If I had organs they'd be falling out of me with the vibrations of my laughter ripping through me.

"Dude, whatever it is you're doing to keep that humor of yours going, promise me you'll keep the secret to yourself. Otherwise, next time I drop in, I'm gonna have a riot on my hands. Anyway, gotta fly. I can hear my theme tune playing." I motion to my skull, referring to the sound of another soul that needs reaping. Death's a greedy bugger, never satisfied.

A shiver runs along my spine like fine hairs tickling my weathered bones. The air compresses around me, squeezing until I become a swirl of black mist again, my wings flapping eagerly.

I zip around the Infernum, missing walls and dodging streams of lava as I break the speed barriers whilst ascending with purpose, leaving the bleak abyss behind.

This place is no holiday destination.

A high-pitched squeal cripples my wings, and I fall, clutching the sides of my skull as pain radiates all over. I forget my flight, the urge to answer a soul's calling taking a back seat. I can't think through the agony the squeals bring. It's like my bones are being pulverized, one small section at a time as though to prolong my despair.

I'm barely aware of how fast I'm falling, how quickly fire and stone walls are now looming over me.

I pull at my skull, desperate to keep the noise from assaulting me further. My efforts bring zero comfort. It's futile, and yet, like a fucking idiot, I can't stop searching for a reprieve, like a magical mute button's going to appear on my cranium.

A sense of foreboding engulfs every inch of me, like darkness is claiming me.

"Shit!" I smack the ground with such force, it's inadvertently become my submissive. On the plus side, the pain's gone, but that's only because I've become completely numb. I'm like a Halloween pinup. Tape me to the front door, and I'll rattle the window in the wind, swinging to and fro like a puppet without strings.

"How nice it is to see you, Shade."

Shit, I inwardly groan. "Well, you know, I thought it was about time I drop in to see the big boss." I keep my distance from the tall entity in front of me.

"Don't bullshit me. Your worthiness is on the line."

I gulp, keeping my mouth shut for fear I'll say something stupid, like another pun that goes unnoticed.

"You fucked up good." Death's dark stare drives fear into my essence. I can feel terror imprinting on my bones. The otherworldly being is like a giant in size and always has his skeletal frame smartly dressed in an array of tailored suits. Besides his height, I'm sure shopping for such clothing is pretty easy. After all, he's never gonna be more than a size zero. Catwalk models would envy our figures—I hear stick-thin is in this season.

At this moment, Death's wearing his favorite onyx suit, as he likes to call it. Honestly, I don't get the bloody color names myself. I see no difference in tones. Black is black, no matter its sale-savvy description. And don't even get me started on the stupid thorned stem he's got peeking out of his pocket. There's no flower head, of course. Nothing can live with Death around. Literally. He really brings out the lack of life in the room.

Shit, he's crossed his bones over his chest, squaring shoulders he doesn't have—the suit does the work for him.

"You don't have anything to tell me? Some remorse perhaps?"

At what point am I supposed to blow his anger up by saying I don't understand to what he's referring?

Oh bollocks, I'm going to cease to exist.

"How many imbeciles do I have to employ to collect souls and get the job done? It's not fucking difficult!" Death roars, temper raging as he kicks out at the tall stands holding flames that illuminate the otherwise dark space. Fire scatters on the concrete ground, burning everything in its path, including my feet. It's a good thing I don't have any skin.

"Dude, you need to tone it down. I've been reaping souls perfectly. In fact, I just dropped another into the Infernum."

Death leans down, putting his hand in front of me. It's as large as my body. With finger and thumb he flicks me hard, sending me across the room until I hit a wall that stops me.

"Don't you fucking 'dude' me, arsehole. This is my place you're fucking with." He stomps toward me. Two steps is all it takes for him to lift me until his large skull is in front of me, mouth opening as though he's going to eat me. I don't know why—the only thing I'm good for is picking meat out of his teeth *after* dinner. "You allowed some souls to escape the goddamn Infernum!"

Death's breath wafts in my face like a gale-force wind. Shit, pass the dead guy a breath mint; he smells worse than a sewer.

"When?" I can't help the shock creeping into my voice. This is news to me. Wouldn't I know if someone left the Infernum? Despite the fact it's bloody impossible in the first place. This has to be some lame joke he's trying to pull on me—the big guy never can match my comedy.

"Not ten minutes ago. While you were busy chatting with our long-term patrons, they were distracting you from the miscreants using the portal you opened to get there. Now they're running free again. Only this time with even less of a conscience." Death's hand smacks me across the other side of the room. I struggle to stand, mostly out of fear of being flung around the room again. This shit hurts.

Did the bear shifter really sell me out? Sapphire I can understand. That bitch always has something brewing in her conniving mind. It's what sent her into the pits of the Infernum in the first place.

"I'll bring them back," I vow, slowly rising to my feet like a beaten man. When Death hits you, you know you're going down for good.

"You'd fucking better, especially the one that orchestrated this whole plan." Though he doesn't have any eyebrows, I imagine Death's scowling at me right now. The dark abyss of his eyes promises loneliness and pain if I fail to deliver.

I try straightening my cloak, brushing off the dust and flames I picked up from my acquaintance with the ground.

"Just out of curiosity, who's the evil mastermind behind all of this?"

Death smiles widely, leaning back into the throne he spends most of his time in. "Nyx, the vampire-demon hybrid. Bring them all back before they cause even more damage to the world."

I nod, knowing I have a lot of work on my hands—Nyx had been tough to capture the first time. I turn, opening up a new portal, where it will lead me to a damned soul's location. As a reaper, it's like I have my own tracking system—the souls call to me whether they know it or not.

"Oh, and Shade, one last thing. If you fuck this up even more, and fail to deliver Nyx to me personally, you're done. No more privileges. No more slack. No more wings. I'll disintegrate your existence."

I close my eyes, taking in the severity of the situation. Just as I step into the portal, I hear Death chuckle. "Good luck!"

CHAPTER 3

HAVENWOOD FALLS

J'm sucked into a whirlwind that throws me about, spinning me one way only to jolt me the other. Time disappears through this vacuum as I'm transported to my next calling. It's not easy to think in this space either, with pressure pushing in on all sides of my body, squeezing me through the fabric of two dimensions. An invisible force tugs me to the right, and I know this is my exit. It's like an instinct. A hole opens up for a split second, and I slip through with ease, popping out of the portal with a zap.

I hover in the sky, a black swirl of mist in the bright blue azure. Closing my eyes, I let the soul reach out to me, waiting for it to tug me in the right direction. With speed on my side, I descend, knowing I need to get my bearings. As a reaper, there are few places I have yet to visit. Perks of the job. Actually, its only perk really. Death isn't exactly the cheeriest guy to work for.

Thankfully, I go unnoticed once I land on my feet, due to my ability to become invisible; can't have any townies glaring at my form —they'd be screaming nonstop. I know, ladies, I'm just that sexy. Everyone wants to jump my bones.

"Hot Cocoa and Cookie Crawl! Come taste the best in the West!" A loud female voice comes from the opposite side of the road. Bodies are moving all over this small town. Surprisingly, I don't recognize it, but based on the accents alone, I know I'm in America. There's no mistaking the twang in those words.

"Come join in the fun! Hot cocoa and cookies all around town for today only! Judge them all until you can't stomach any more!"

Intrigued, I cross the road and step into the crowd. I love this part. I'm like a ninja, moving around without interference. No one sees me coming until it's too late. I'm a bad omen like that.

"You! What are you doing here? Why are you in Havenwood Falls?"

I take a step back. This girl's gotta be trippin'. There's no way she can see me. I step aside—she has to be referring to whoever's behind me.

"Reaper, I'm talking to you. Why are you here?"

Well, fuck me. How the hell can she see me? "You know, you probably look really crazy right now, talking to thin air."

"You have a British accent," she says as though this surprises her, but then she shrugs and grabs my arm. We're instantly transported to the inside of a building. It's empty, save for a reception area. There's no indication as to what kind of work place this is. Interesting. This girl's got me curious.

"What are you?" I scent the air, picking up the strength of magic exuding from the woman, but there's something else, something that matches the attitude of her attire. Ripped jeans, slogan T-shirt, leather jacket, beanie hat. What is she?

"What I am is not your concern, but why you're here is mine. Explain yourself."

Who the hell does this broad think she is, ordering me around? Angels of Death take orders from one person only, and even then that's only out of fear. The guy literally has the power to keep us in the ground for good. This girl has nothing on me.

"I'm working. I go where the souls call from. Seeing as you know what I am, I'm disappointed you didn't figure that out already." I lean against the long reception desk, commanding the space as my own. She doesn't rattle me.

"Nobody's died here. Try again."

I smirk. "I didn't know you knew everything and everyone in this town to be so clued in on who's alive." I cross my arms over my skeletal frame. I'm going to have fun messing with her.

"Actually, I do. This isn't like any other place you've visited before."

I guffaw. "Yeah, okay, princess. Who made you ruler of the land? Towns, no matter how many you visit, are all the same. The only thing that changes are the names. You still have your quirky shops, necessary businesses, park, school, church, graveyard, and emergency services. Please, stop me if I'm wrong."

She shakes her head. "No, you're just missing one crucial element, something I'm amazed you haven't figured out yet, you know, considering your *job*."

I slouch onto the desk, letting her tell me everything I need to know. "Go on then. Tell me what makes this town stand out amongst all others?"

She leans forward, whispering into my ear. "It's a supernatural town. Practically equal in the supe to human ratio."

I shrug, nonplussed. Whatever species live here, it makes no difference to my job—I take all souls, once their time has come. "Great, and how does this explain how you supposedly know whether a soul needs reaping or not? You got magic dibs on everyone?"

"Something like that. This town has its own Court and rules, something the founders set up to keep track of and protect the residents here. This place is special and a haven for many."

"Okay, princess. But you still haven't answered my question. Why does it matter if I'm here?"

She huffs loudly, as though resigning herself to a long tale. If only I had popcorn and a seat. These ol' bones are getting creaky.

"We make all supernatural creatures register with the Court. It's a way to protect them and us. And the town is warded too, so the second you step foot in our borders, we know. So, reaper, who are you here for? And don't even think about giving me vague answers. There's too much shit going on to waste time on you."

I chuckle. "Glad to know I'm of importance." This place has me even more intrigued. How did I not know of it before? In my circles, a town laden with supernatural creatures would rank high as a conversation topic. I certainly want to find out more. I consider my options and decide on absolute honesty. What's it gonna hurt? "Some souls escaped the Infernum. I'm here to collect."

"The Infernum? *Again?* Are you fucking kidding me? Who are they? It'd better not be that damn Indrori!" She narrows her eyes, and if looks could scorn, I'd be burning up right now.

Well, shit. That's it—her missing piece! "You're a hellhound."

She quickly scans the empty room. "*Half* hellhound, thank you, and I'd appreciate it if you kept that to yourself. Let's get back on track. These souls—are they going to cause a problem here? I can't have them running amok. The Court will have to intercept."

"Whoa, whoa, whoa. Hold your horses there, princess. This is my job, not this Court or special town's. I don't have names." *Except for one*, I keep to myself. There's no reason to reveal all my dirty laundry to this stranger. "You're just gonna have to let me get on with it, and then I'll happily leave this place behind."

"If you even think you're hanging around here for more than five minutes without registering and having a temporary tattoo done before walking out, then you're mistaken. You might be a reaper, and you might work for Death, but trust will have to be earned. There's too much crap going on right now as it is, especially with the Collec—"

I lean forward, goading her to say more. Unfortunately, she chooses this moment to exercise her silence. Bugger.

"Is that why you're here? You're reaping for the Collector?" She pounces on me out of the blue.

I frown. "I have no idea who you're talking about. I work for Death. All reapers work for him only. Who's this Collector?"

"If you're not working for him, then you must know something about him from all your visits to the different realms. What can you tell me?"

I stare at her, dumbfounded. "Honestly, you sound like a crazy person. What are you talking about?"

She stares hard, frowning with suspicion, but doesn't offer any insight to this madness.

I sigh, exasperated. "Look, you got shit to deal with. So have I. So let's adjourn this meeting and get back to the important stuff. Besides, I'm not sure why you think a tattoo's going to help any, especially when I have no canvas to present." I lift the cloak up my arms, showing off my bony digits, ulna, and radius. I turn to leave, but once again, the sassy hell witch grabs my arm and keeps me pinned to the wall with an invisible force field. I'll give it to her—the girl's got some balls trying to restrain a being like me. We're not exactly the cuddly-bear, forgiving kind.

"Don't make me repeat myself, reaper. I won't let you careen around without being seen. You will be tattooed until the Court decides what to do with you."

I roll my eyes. Again she bangs on about a bloody tattoo. Am I missing something here? I have nothing a needle can penetrate, let alone stain. Stupid little girl. Sodding idiots are everywhere these days.

With the magical grip she has on me, I struggle to escape, but there's a lot more strength in her than meets the eye.

"The tattoo will make you appear human, fill you out a little more." She motions to my lack of shape. "And yes, that means you'll have to wear clothes like the rest of us, eat, and sleep. And depending on your time scale, if you stick around long enough, you may even experience a few desires." She winks.

"No offense, princess. You don't do it for me, you're too . . ."

"Talented? Beautiful? Enigmatic? Doesn't matter anyway, I'm spoken for."

I grin widely, having scented the answer to this question earlier. "By a vampire, yes. Unfortunately for you, I don't do blood bag leftovers."

"Fuuuck, do you ever shut up? You must drive Death to insanity with this incessant chit-chat. Fuck knows how he puts up with you."

I shrug. She doesn't need to know of the tensions between the boss and me. She turns for the desk, leaving me to hover in the room's entryway. I watch her rummage in one of the drawers.

"Perfect. This will do. You got any picture preference or are you giving me free rein?" She lifts the gun in her hands, squeezing until the needle buzzes a few times. "Great, artist's choice it is."

As hard as I try I'm still unable to move, which works well for the witch as she lifts the cloak from my right arm and lets the needle push against the top of my right humerus. There's no pain, just an annoying itch-like scratch I can't touch. Christ, it's irritating.

"Can we hurry this along please? I've got some wall-staring to get to."

"The Court will want to have words with you."

"I thought you were the Court," I counter, watching as she puts her tattoo kit away, back in the drawer behind the reception desk.

"I'm just their business manager. I'm sure you can appreciate this town is too big for one supe to manage alone, let alone the fact it wouldn't be very democratic."

"How very civilized," I quip, having seen my fair share of savage supernaturals, and that's without them intermingling. Too many creatures consider themselves purists, and to even acknowledge another species is a big sin. These crazy motherfuckers make life interesting.

"Okay, when I let you go, the tattoo will take effect, and you'll change. No more invisibility for you until you're on a reaping hunt. Then, and only then, will you change forms while you're in Havenwood Falls, got it?"

I nod. There's not much more to say.

"Then I need to register you. A drop of blood, and your name, and you can get out of my hair for the day."

I burst into laughter, and the bubble-like barrier wrapped around my middle jiggles from the movement. "Princess, I don't have any blood to give you. I'm literally bone dry."

She stares upwards, putting hands to hips as if searching for some kind of strength. "You'll have a human form soon enough, and as that's the one meandering around town, the blood markers will do. Are you really this stupid? Do I need to explain every small thing to you? Do you know how to reap a soul or should I demonstrate the ins and outs of that too?"

This girl is no fun. She's deflated my happy buzz. "Fine, I'll give you my name if you give me yours."

"That is such a cheesy line. You want to score around here, you'll have to work harder." She clicks her fingers, and I fall, landing clumsily on my bones. "I'm Addie. You'll get used to seeing me around, and trust me when I say we'll be watching you."

"Well, Addie, I'm Shade StormIron. It's a pleasure to meet you," I say sarcastically. She grabs my hand once more and pricks my thumb —I'm no longer just bones. I didn't even feel the change. How unusual.

"Don't thank me yet, Shade. You haven't seen what you look like now."

Well, shit. I bet she's made me some old, fat bastard. Crap.

CHAPTER 4

HELLHOUNDS

"*H*ey, handsome, wanna taste my hot cocoa?"

"If it's as good as you look, then we're on to a winner." I give the woman my cheekiest smile and wink. She blushes in response. She's pretty, but there's no real interest in her brown eyes. She's just after a quick sale, and I'm almost inclined to give it to her. What the fuck is wrong with me? It has to be the human skin, right? It's making me soft. Stupid bloody rules. Of all the places the souls could've gone, why here? And how the hell have they gone unnoticed? The second my feet hit the ground here, I had Princess all over me. Something isn't right.

I make my way through the town. It looks like Santa's jizzed all over the place. There's a bloody huge tree, no doubt modelled after his own penis size, and twinkling lights everywhere. Everywhere. I'm amazed they haven't found their way into my hair. Yeah, I have bloody hair now, and it's goddamn gorgeous too, if the reflection I keep catching in shop windows is anything to go by. Never mind the stares from the thirsty locals. Yeah, baby, they want the D I'm packing. "Hey, babe, do you know what a compressed file is? You'd better unzip my pants to find out."

"Ew, gross!"

I turn away, laughing to myself. Serves her right. The ugly woman standing in front of the coffee shop window thought I was checking her out, when actually, I've just been admiring my new look. It's a lot to get used to. To begin with, I have skin. Tight skin that covers big, muscular arms and torso. I seem to be of the same six-foot-plus height, thankfully. And now I've got the perfect smolder. People can finally appreciate my charisma.

"Sir, have you tried our cookies?" A young girl comes up to me, blue eyes gazing at me through long eyelashes in the most adorable way. My heart almost skips a beat, she's that precious, holding out her hands with a cellophane bag of decorated cookies gift wrapped with a ribbon. Oh, boy, the shop owners have done well, using this bundle of innocence to coerce even the hardest of me out of my money.

Shit! Do I even have money?

My stomach starts to growl, reminding me I'm susceptible to human needs now. Fuck me, this is going to slow me down exponentially. Why this bloody town? That's it. It's decided. Death truly does hate me.

"She got you good, man. Don't break her little heart now."

I shake my head to the stranger, though I recognize him as a hellhound. Why else would you wear sunglasses when it's a dull day?

"Dude, you have no idea. I'm Shade." I hold out a hand, waiting for the fellow to introduce himself. We're of the same height and build, and I can sense the wildness in him, his second nature.

"Ace," he replies, gripping my hand firmly. It's not until he touches my skin that he realizes who I am. Although the Infernum is a massive abyss, there are times when I bump into hellhounds there. Ace isn't one of them.

"You sticking around?" He raises a brow, crossing a fully tattooed arm over the other.

I shrug. There's no real answer that offers a probable timeframe here. "Until the job is done. There's always another calling, speaking of which . . ." My spine tingles into awareness, like cold hands reaching out to me.

"Later, man. You should check out the club; you may find

someone you know." Ace tilts his head to the left, I'm assuming as a means of direction to this so-called club.

I disappear, finding my chance to escape now that the cookie-selling girl is preoccupied with conning a loved-up couple out of their money. Suckers.

My feet, now kitted out in swanky brown Timberland boots, command my body around the town, guiding me to the soul that's calling.

It's going to take me forever in this monkey suit. What the hell am I gonna do? *Oh, sorry, Death. I couldn't catch the souls in time because this fucked up mystical town made me human, stunting all efficiency. Please don't punish me further. This clearly isn't my fault. Signed, Shade.*

I snort to myself, as if that shit would ever wash.

I'm so caught up in my self-pity monologue that I don't even notice day switching to night. My stomach still grumbles, too.

"Well, what do we have here?"

I blink a few times, struggling to make sense of where I am. I'm standing in a parking lot, at the base of one of the box canyon's mountains. A big beefy bodyguard stands by what I can only describe as a gondola-shaped lift. Where the bloody hell am I? Town isn't around here, and people seem to have disappeared. Fucking excellent. This soul is leading me into some mafia's lair, I can feel it.

"What is this?" I point to the tall cave-like edifice, where the gondolas ascend. I wonder where they lead to.

"Got an invitation?" The guy huffs, ignoring my question completely. Instead, he's now preoccupied with some overly smartly dressed men and women. He checks them out, scanning the paper one member of the party hands over. What is this? Some secret club for the rich? I snort internally, having now witnessed it all.

Beefy Bodyguard sends them on their way, into the lift that takes them up and to a place I know I'm supposed to be.

"You. No invitation, no admittance. Private Christmas party tonight. It's that simple."

This guy is pissing me off. Everyone here is so sodding nosy. I don't take shit from anyone, especially not some jacked-up guy throwing his muscle around. We can all be dicks like that; some of us choose not to be. Tosser.

"I don't give a shit." I get up in his face, seeing my own reflection in the glasses he's wearing. "Fuck me, is this place riddled with hellhounds?"

Princess had me believing this is a place for species to coexist. So far, I've only met one kind—goddamn hellhounds, with their skewed self-important view of the world.

"Watch what you're talking about. You don't mess with us. Now go."

I shake my head. "Nope. Come on, big fella, aren't you even a little curious as to who I am? I mean, I totally just outed you. Care to retaliate?"

He pushes my shoulders, attempting to get me out of his face. He stops short, hands recoiling as though I've burnt him. Don't even get me started on the irony of that.

"Problem?" I smirk, knowing I've finally got his full attention.

"What are you doing here, reaper? And why the hell do you look like this?" He lifts his shades, knowing his eyes won't affect me. A hellhound's eyes are notorious for killing—look in them three times and you're frazzled. Not me, though. Death is my master.

"Witch bitch wouldn't let me walk around this place without a skin suit. Now, back to why I came. I gotta get in there." I point to the mysterious entrance above in the cave.

He shakes his head. I don't believe it. "Can't do that. Melaina will fucking kill me. There's no trouble here."

This guy is seriously testing my patience now. "You can say all you want, but when a soul calls my name, I can't walk away. You should know this." I give him my most disappointed stare. "I'm getting in there with or without your help."

"What soul?" The guy squares up to me, clearly assuming I'm telling one big lie to get involved in whatever the secret space is hiding up there. Obviously, based on the party earlier, money can get you in. Is this some kind of cage-fighting joint? One off the books for legal reasons?

"One that escaped the fucking Infernum. Are we done, or do I have to knock you out now?"

The guy blares out with laughter. Excellent. Nice to know I've tickled his pickle. Bloody time waster.

"If there's trouble, Melaina will sort it. You won't be going up."

I pull back a fist, pushing forward for the smug grin on his face. He grabs my fist before I connect with flesh, and thrusts a punch directly at my nose, the large mass expanding to fit my forehead too. Guy's got big hands.

I stagger back, dazed and confused as the dark night swirls around me. I hit the ground and zone out, darkness taking me.

20

CHAPTER 5

SONG

"*I* think you broke him. He's been out too long. Doesn't look like his skin suit is strong enough to handle a reaper."

I keep my eyes closed for a few more minutes, fooling these strangers to gain the advantage. Mentally, I take note of any injuries, working from my head down. My nose is sore but other than that, I'm fine, but they don't need to know it. Winning battles always comes to whoever has the upper hand—I'm not about to reveal all my cards, especially as I don't know where I'm at, or whose company I'm now keeping.

My stomach chooses this moment to let out a wail like it's being stabbed to death; probably reckons my throat's been cut too. Stupid human needs.

"Well, shit," I exhale, sitting up. It's difficult to lie still when your belly's roar takes on a life of its own. "Don't suppose you've got some food stashed in that skinny dress?"

I forget introductions and wariness. Man can concentrate only on his gut when it demands sustenance. I'm tempted to click my fingers at the sexy brunette staring at me, just to piss her off some more, but for once, I think better of the idea and take on a polite persona. I know, it's bloody sickening behavior, but the hellhound just won't shake a leg fast enough.

How are there more hellhounds in this mysterious town than there are in the Infernum? Clearly they don't respect their roles. They're everywhere.

My neck tingles, the sensation trailing along my spine like an attack of angry birds pecking at my spinal column. It's bloody uncomfortable, to say the least. I leave the room, ignoring the protests being shouted behind me. Step by step, the pain becomes more of an irritation, reducing as a means of navigation the closer I get.

"What the hell do you think you're doing?"

Why does everyone keep asking me this?

The female hound stands in front of me as though her small frame is enough to stop me. I scowl.

"Shut up." I try halting the loud tones of her voice from spooking this soul away. "It's here." I scoot around her, peering around the corner of a room that's booming music with little care to noise levels.

True to the witch's word, my form changes of its own accord. I have no control over it. Skin disappears until I'm only bones, and I can feel my wings emerging, stretching out of my back like they've been trapped for far too long.

I take on a black mist as I swirl into the air, entering the room without being seen as I hover through the crowd undetected. I have *all* my abilities at work now.

The damned soul calls to me, like there's a bright red beacon illuminating my target. Without hesitation I speed to the mirage of a man, unwilling to let him escape my grasp. There's nothing innocent or human about this projection—it's just the form the soul wants you to see.

In an instant we slam through a portal to the Infernum, ignoring all conversations thrown my way. I'm not going to be distracted this time.

"Shit!" I snap at myself, recognizing the couch area I've just tumbled into. Of all the sodding places the portal could've opened . . .

"Back so soon, reaper? We need to set some rules." The female hellhound maneuvers around her desk at the opposite end of the room. "Now, this club is mine to protect. I can't have you waltzing your way in whenever you want. I don't give a shit if there's a soul here. If it's not causing trouble, it can party its ass off. Got it? No. Scenes. Here."

I sit back on the couch, resting my feet on the coffee table, folding arms behind my head. Yeah, she's pissed. Heels clack on the floor.

"Don't you have any fucking respect?"

"Listen, babe. We know who I work for. It's not like I can just walk away from a soul. That's not how this works. If another ends up here, I'm gonna have to come regardless of your opinion. I'm surprised, Ms. . . ."

"Melaina Savage," she supplies.

I nod. "Shade," I point to myself. "I would've thought escapees from the Infernum would worry you."

She shrugs, relaxing enough to take one of the seats. "It does, but that's secondary to what else is going on in this town right now."

I lean forward, seeing an opportunity. "Then why don't we come to an agreement. You give me free rein in this place, and I promise to be incognito when reaping. Deal?"

She narrows her eyes. "How can you guarantee that?"

"Did anyone notice me earlier?" I raise a brow, letting the corners of my mouth lift in satisfaction. I already know the answer.

"Fine, but you don't speak of anything that happens here. Privacy is our guarantee."

I stand. "Don't worry, Melaina. I'll wear you down soon enough, and you'll start loving me." I pause, smiling. "By the way, what else has got everyone so uptight in this town? You all seem to want to deal with me, yet no one wants to spare the time." I wait, but she doesn't give in. What's going in on in this town? I sigh. "See you around, hottie. I'm being bugged again." I wink, leaving the room via the door this time.

I make my way to the lower levels, becoming more ensconced in caverns the more I descend. If I were a decent enough guy, I'd even compliment Ms. Savage on a job well done. There's certainly an allure here, whether it's the moody atmosphere produced by low lighting or the separation of rooms offering different experiences. And fuck me, some are definitely more lively than others. Lively enough I bet it's cause enough to make even Death blush.

My new, annoying stomach grumbles again, reminding me how well I've adapted to this new body. Neglect is a forte of mine. But all of that fades into the background when a song, the most enchanting piano melody, slow and seductive, calls to me in a way I've never felt before. This isn't an uncomfortable tingle along my spine where some soul is in need of direction to the right afterlife zone. This is the kind of awakening that makes me feel alive, desperate to clutch and never release. It's full of joy and promise, building excitement within me.

Listen to me babbling on like some new-age, life-is-everything guru. This body is making me soft. There's no other explanation for it.

"Can I get you a drink, handsome?"

I'm pulled from my thoughts when a blonde speaks, notepad in hand, skin more visible than clothing. Without a doubt, this party cavern is screaming sex.

"What do you recommend?" I cast it off as light flirtation, but really I have no bloody clue what tastes good. I've not had the pleasure of taste buds before, or the need to use them. It's like I'm that puppet who becomes a real boy. At least he always had wood. So far mine seems as nonexistent as it's always been. It's like a sad elephant down there.

"You know, you look to me like you're here for a surprise. Do you trust me?"

I shrug, giving the waitress the go-ahead. I'm too distracted to really care anyway. It's not a drink that's going to be wetting my whistle right now.

Who is that?

I hear the melody in my mind again, tender piano notes trickling through. If I didn't know any better, I'd say this instant reaction is the work of a mating partnering up. Too bad I know that kind of life isn't in store for me. After all, who's ever heard of a reaper getting a happily ever after? No, fairytale love doesn't exist—I'm destined for the sorrow of soul reaping only. There's no plus-one ticket where I'm heading. And this packaging I'm flaunting right now won't be around forever. I'll be back to bare bones the moment I leave this place. It's not exactly the warm and comforting body women want to snuggle up to at night. And let's face it, my figure will always be a bone of contention. Compared to me, they'll always look fat. It's not my fault God gave them organs and Death gave me a hollow shell. I'm just pointing out the facts. Anyway, who the hell has time for pointless, illogical arguments?

Fuck me. If the reaction I'm currently having is any indication, then I know what's about to happen. I'm screwed. More importantly, my cock is now pointing the way. I've suddenly become a testosterone-filled, puberty-ripe teenager. How the hell do I control this thing? Look at it—it's like a chubby baby's arm is waving around, looking for a response.

It's all *her* fault too—the woman in the center of the room, twirling her body around a long pole. Small pieces of red fabric barely cover her tits and arse, with heels that accentuate long, toned legs. I want to pin her against the bar wall, let everyone see as I claim her, running my tongue all over her body, satiating this uncontrollable thirst that's currently consuming me. I want to take her nipples into my mouth, watch as she arches her back with desire.

An unsubtle cough catches my attention. The waitress from before has impeccable timing.

"Your drink. It's a screw-me-six-ways cocktail. You look like you need it." She winks, glancing at the massive bulge I'm barely concealing in my jeans. She disappears before I have time to form a rebuke, and I'm back to fantasizing about my time with this dancer.

The club disappears as she becomes my sole focus. She pulls me in like she's got me on a leash, tugging for me to come closer. My feet move without my brain sending signals. I'm not in control of my own body. This song that still calls out to me seems to be dictating my movements.

Even from across the room, I knew this woman was beautiful, but up close, she takes my breath away. Breath I very much need to rely on

25

in this town. She twirls some more, contorting her body around the thin metal cylinder. Beautiful long black hair cascades over her back, shining in the spotlight illuminating her. The music is coming to an end, and she slows to the rhythm, her routine over with the last note.

This is when I know I'm fucked. Her eyes meet mine, and pools of bright blue have me drowning inside them. I'm lost in their sparkling depth.

"Take a picture. It might last longer." She winks, moving to leave the elevated stage she's been dancing on.

"Wait, what's your name, beautiful?"

She hangs back, almost as though my question has startled her. "Why?"

"Because I'd like to think of the name that matches this pretty face." I cringe at the corny line coming out of my mouth. My smooth-guy ability has evacuated the building. She laughs, and I'm drawn further to her beautiful being. She's got me wrapped around her little finger.

She leans forward, her scent of flowers surrounding me.

"Thalia Prince," she whispers, then leaves, giving me the perfect view of her arse swaying with each step.

Bollocks. I want her.

CHAPTER 6

SCREWED

*H*er lips linger on mine, a taste of something sweet and spicy. Foods I've yet to try tingle my tongue like electricity sparking between us. It sends my body into overdrive, and I desperately need more.

"Thalia," I exhale, loving the way her name rolls off my tongue like it's mine to keep.

"What do you want from me, Shade?" Her lips purse, swollen from the friction of my own. Hell yeah, I like this. It raises a carnality in me.

I lean in, our faces barely a breath apart as I stare into her enchanting eyes. "I want you to bare your soul to me."

She moves swiftly, wrapping her jeans-covered legs around my waist, arms around my neck. I cup her juicy arse, gripping tightly as I claim her lips once again. Her tongue battles with mine, a duel of passion exchanging between us. I can't get enough; she doesn't feel close enough.

Her hands tangle in my hair, driving me wild. I pin her against a wall, letting her feel the length of my cock desperate to be freed.

I tear at her shirt like a savage beast, and strips of fabric are all that remain, scattered on the floor at my feet. I wait for some argument about her having some emotional attachment to the shirt, but she surprises me. My hunger's ignited her own, and now she's tearing into mine, grabbing the tight-fitting cotton stretched over my broad shoulders and chest. She huffs with aggravation, struggling to pry the top from my skin. If I wasn't so fucking horny for her right now, I'd consider the pout on her face fucking adorable. But I'm not a soppy bastard.

I stare at the sparkly black bra she's wearing, enhancing the beautiful shape of her bouncy boobs. Shit yeah, they jiggle like perfectly set jelly.

I can't wait any more. There's nothing left of my patience. I need to hear her screaming my name out, over and over like I'm the god she worships. I set her down on my bed, practically ripping the jeans hugging her arse and baring silky skin that's calling to my lips.

"What are you looking at, Shade?" Her voice comes out on a heavy breath, lust lighting up her eyes like beautiful Christmas decorations. She can be the angel on the top of my tree any time she wants, as long as she's naked.

"How much I want to make you come." I wiggle my brows, liking the pink blush that warms her cheeks. How can she look so innocent after I've seen her dance at the club?

My cock is pulsing so rapidly, it's about to take off like a rocket. Hot fluid coming at you in 3 . . . 2 . . . 1 . . .

Thalia runs her hands over my arms, my biceps flexing as I hover over her, framing her body with my own. She looks so delicate and fierce at the same time.

"Fuck me, Shade. Let me forget."

I don't need her to tell me twice. I trail my tongue along her neck, over the top of her breasts while I free them from their fabric cage. I take her perky nipple into my mouth, suckling the already hard bud. She moans in response, arching her back for more.

Her hands grip the sheets as I continue exploring her body, reaching her hips. With each new kiss to her pussy, I pull away the thong, letting her spread her legs wide, cunt completely exposed to my waiting mouth. Fuck me, even her scent has me salivating like Daffy Duck.

"Shade," she moans in anticipation; that voice almost makes me give in and shag her senseless, but I want this to last. She isn't a five minute happy for me. No, I want at least a week. I want to come all over her the way the snow lays on the ground.

I flick her clit with my tongue, letting her absorb the feeling before doing it again, but fuck me, I want to devour her already. Her pussy juices coat my tongue like the sweetest elixir.

"Oh, God, Shade. Again," she calls. Her hand fists in my hair, and I feel her legs tighten either side of my head as I swirl my tongue around her pussy, slipping in a finger, then a second as I pump my hand in and out of her, my tongue lapping at her clit. Her warmth surrounds me, building like an inferno. "Oh, Shade," she moans, breathing deeply. "Shade, I'm going to come. Oh, God . . ."

I pump my fingers harder, work my hand faster until I push her off the edge completely, screaming my name with vigor, zero boundaries between us. "Shade . . ."

I bolt upright, eyes struggling to open, confusion pressing in on me like I've been drugged. I don't understand. Where's Thalia?

"Good morning, Shade. Looks like you had a good night."

I pull the covers up over my body, a raging boner poking the duvet like an obvious beacon. The granny-like figure hovering at the foot of the bed makes zero sense. I try to speak, but between a croaky sleep-heavy voice and an inability to form a full sentence, I'm fucked from the get-go. Where the hell am I?

"Oh, dear, you look so lost. What's troubling you?"

I take a moment to gather my thoughts, sweeping a glance around the room I'm in. There's the bed I'm obviously lying in, a window ahead, though currently with plain curtains drawn. A wardrobe to my left and a desk to my right, and hopefully somewhere around the corner a bathroom, because I'm suddenly needing quite the release. How the hell do humans cope with the constant requirements a body needs? If it's not hunger, it's a drink, and if it's not a drink, it's a piss, then comes tiredness. It's like a hamster wheel of never-ending demands. How do they ever get anything done?

"Are you lost?" I ask the ghostly figure who's currently keeping my company. "Do you need me to take you to the beyond?"

She laughs. "Oh, no, dear. I'm quite all right here."

"Are you sure? I know it can get lonely. Seeing and interacting with people you know here is great, but not having any physical contact at all can leave you empty. I can offer you more than this."

"Thank you, Shade, but really, I'm needed here. I'll call on you if I change my mind."

I sigh, sadness seeping into my skin. It always pains me to see a wandering soul. "How did I get here?" I ask the woman, realizing I don't know her name, though somehow she knows mine. "Ms. . . ."

"You may call me Madame Luiza." She smiles brightly, and I can almost feel it warm the room. This lady must have been remarkable when she was alive. "You stumbled in here last night. You don't remember?"

I think hard, but it's all a blur. The only thing I remember definitively is meeting Thalia.

"You were quite inebriated, young man. Anything could have happened to you."

I laugh at her scorn, young being an adjective I wouldn't give my two hundred plus years. There's very little that can harm a reaper, even when I'm stuck in this meat suit. It may give me certain limitations, but I'm sure if it came down to it, if this body couldn't contain me, regardless of the tattoo and its restrictions, I'm sure I'd return to my usual state of skeleton and cape. Mr. Sexy in all his glory.

"But why am I here?"

"You really don't remember?"

"I think the screw-me-six-ways cocktails have something to do with that."

"Yes, you kept mentioning a beauty you found at Silk."

I can't help but pick up on the disdain in her voice. Is Silk a sore spot for some residents here?

"I'm guessing she directed you here. Not seen you around before, so I'm sure you didn't have anywhere to stay?" She continues to hover, her presence almost becoming a nuisance now. What is the deal with this bloody nightclub? Why all the secrecy and scorn?

Once again I damn the stupidity of human needs. How much precious time have I wasted being distracted by a woman and then spending hours with eyes closed? This isn't productive. Death will take me for sure.

"My niece brought you up here. This is her business. Whisper Falls Inn," Madame Luiza fills in, a wide smile plastering her translucent face as if with pride.

"Great, any souls running amok here? Besides you, of course."

"No, dear. This place is too calm for what you're searching for. You'd have better luck wandering the cemetery." She cackles, disappearing without a goodbye.

Fucking strange. Havenwood Falls is full of unusual characters.

I think about the day ahead, of the countless souls I have yet to track. Why can't I feel them all, calling me forward? I didn't expect to be spending more than one day on this mission—there's more work all around the world to be doing.

I fail to see a bathroom in my room, so I grab my jeans and head into the corridor in search of a communal one. I overhear the tail end of a conversation between two old biddies.

"Blood was pulled from her entire body. Nothing left. Bone dry."

I close my eyes, already knowing the culprit. This town might be filled with an array of supernatural creatures, but I'm certain none would be so careless as to leave a body to be found. No, this comes from someone who doesn't give a shit. And I can think of one major soul that should be calling out to me already.

"Shit," I whisper to myself. "It's Nyx," I continue to mumble to myself, thinking up my next move. A vampire-demon hybrid is bad news, even for a town like this.

CHAPTER 7

ADDICTION

I've never had to consider what it's like to be human. My verdict? It sucks. I'm standing in a long-arse queue in this coffee shop, waiting to get a taste of whatever it is that smells so bloody good in here. I don't even remember making the decision to come in here. It's like an addiction I don't even have forced me this way.

"You know, I hear the sheriff is furious, probably blaming himself if you ask me."

I stay where I am, thankful for at least one good thing about queuing: gossips.

"Why? The poor man can't stop everything going on in this town. It's not like the people expect him to know of a crime before it's committed. Our sheriff puts too much pressure on himself. Ask me, he's a fine man." This old lady winks at her friend, and the pair of them giggle like girls, sniggering at their naughty thoughts.

"It makes me wonder what kind of a monster is living among us. How can a body even be drained of all blood without a drop on the ground or an open wound?"

I have the answers they're looking for, but these humans aren't privy to this side of the Havenwood Falls they live in. If they were, I'm sure they'd be hunting down every vampire that resides in this town, which, oddly enough, includes my current landlady, if my instincts are correct. At least there's more here than bloody hellhounds. Honestly, it's like work just follows me around wherever I end up. I wonder what Death would have to say if I asked for some time off. I inwardly snort at the ridiculous notion. What would I do with time off anyway? What I am is what I do; it's all I've been created for.

"It's lucky they even found her way out in the cemetery like that." Old Lady One finishes her sentences with a case of Tourette-like tuts whilst shaking her head. If she bobs any harder, she'll be snapping her own neck, giving me more work. Selfish cow.

I so desperately want to find out more, but how can I ask without seeming like a creep? It's not like I'm a local, with a vested interest in the people that populate this place. No, I'll only be offering myself up as a great suspect, and something tells me that if I started a conversation with these ladies, I'd never have a chance to leave. It's not that they reek of loneliness. Oh, bollocks, who am I kidding? Of course they're bloody lonely—it's the sole reason anyone gossips in the first place. Honestly, these humans think they're so infallible, when really their basic need for nurturing controls their minds and their actions, too.

"Do you know who she was?"

I lean forward automatically, praying the cashier doesn't call them up next, taking their conversation with them.

"I'm not sure. I can't remember the name now. Oh, I'm sure it'll come back to me soon; just need some java to kick-start the old brain." Old Lady One taps her noggin. "Unless it's one of the many tourists." At the same time, they both turn to look at me with knowing glances. Thankfully, the cashier's now free.

I stare at the menu board, ignoring the oldies now that I've managed to spark their interest with my presence. I read the menu again and again. Cappuccino. Latte. Flat white. Americano. What the hell is the difference anyway? I thought coffee is coffee. How can there be so many kinds? How am I supposed to know which one I'll like best?

I've heard humans talk about the drink for decades, but not once have they ever mentioned it comes in a variety! Why do they do this to themselves? Aren't their lives complicated enough without being quizzed on what type of coffee bean to milk to water ratio they want?

Wait a minute, what's this? I squint at the board some more, reading further. Christ, you have to decide what milk you want? What. The. Fuck. MILK IS MILK! What's with all these weird options? Almond, coconut, soya. I did not realize how insane the world has become. It's no wonder they're so bloody miserable most of the time. And why am I so hung up on this that I'm giving it valuable thinking time? Shit, this is it. This is how it sucks you in. *Welcome to coffee roulette. Here's your loyalty card for all offers to keep you coming back, you addict.*

What am I doing? I give up as the cashier calls me forward. I'm not here for these social pleasures. I grasp the door handle just as it's being pushed in my direction, and I freeze. Luscious black locks and bright blue eyes hold me still; sweet and spicy invade my senses, and I love it. Her scent is everything I need to bring me comfort.

"Thalia," I whisper, flashes of this morning's horny dreams filling my mind, and I'm instantly having to control my cock from making headline news.

She frowns, standing half in and half out of Coffee Haven. "Do I know you?"

Fuck me, it's like a dagger to my new heart, slashed around for extra pain.

"We met last night, at the club," I add, considering she's still staring with a blank face. My ego is not faring well here. I'm clearly not the only hunk she's crossed paths with; and here I've been thinking I'm quite the memorable guy. Shit, this interaction business is brutal. At least when I'm reaping it's all banter—what're a skeleton and a soul gonna do? Talk about bumping uglies. But this, here with Thalia, can lead to so much more, if only my cock will let me do the talking. Down, boy.

"Yes, you're the one they renamed the cocktail after."

I raise a brow. "They did?"

She nods emphatically, a smile covering her gorgeous face. "Yup, a Rookie Reaper."

If I had a drink right now, it would be pouring out of my nostrils. This cocktail name business sounds more like an insult than flattery—and if the hellhound boss had anything to do with it, I'm sure that's her intention. Savage by name *and* nature.

"Why would they do that?"

"Your drinks last night were new, so . . ."

I can tell she thinks I'm stupid. Her face says it all with the raised lip. If expressions can talk, this one is *I can't believe you're such an idiot.* I need to remedy this quickly.

"She told me it was called a screw me six ways."

Thalia bursts into laughter, struggling to compose herself. "She was messing with you. Six liquors were in it, but the rest . . . Well, let's just say she noticed you had a situation to solve." Thalia blushes, now avoiding my gaze. "They were considering calling it the British Invasion but decided against it—even though you have the weird accent, you don't actually come from there, do you?"

I shake my head. I seem to get this a lot on my travels. "When you've been to as many places as I have, there are certain phrases and pronunciations that stick." I shrug it off as though it's no big deal. I don't even pay attention to what I say anymore. It just comes naturally.

I realize we're still blocking the coffee shop's doorway, me half out, and her half in.

"Come on, let me buy you a cup of coffee, and you can tell me about the club." I grasp her shoulder gently, urging her toward me.

She slams her arm down on mine, breaking the connection. Her eyes are wide, feral, and her face has become pale.

"Don't ever touch me again!" she roars, back ramrod straight before she turns and runs away, leaving me highly perplexed.

What the hell just happened?

I take a quick glance around the coffee shop, noting a few faces glaring at me, the others too engaged in their own conversations to care.

Without another thought, I chase after her, running through the town in a confused daze. I replay the moment over in my mind, wondering what I did wrong.

Did my touch really hurt her this much? I have to know why.

CHAPTER 8

PAST

*E*ven with the snow-covered ground and frigid temperatures, I'm still sweating, beads cooling instantly along my back like icy barnacles.

I see Thalia just past the water fountain, sitting in the gazebo, surrounded by the white stuff. Gone is the woman I saw dancing last night, confidence emanating from her skin. Here, I see a shy, broken lady weeping with sadness. I don't know why, but even from afar it stirs a protective hunger in me. I want to take her pain away, beat up the arsehole who did this to her.

I inch slowly, afraid she'll run away from me again. "Thalia, whatever I did, I'm sorry. I didn't mean to hurt you if I gripped too hard. You see, I'm still getting used to this—"

"It wasn't you," she interrupts, eyes glassy with tears unshed. "I overreacted."

I shake my head. I know there's more to it than that. Her reaction was too reflexive for there to not be a bigger problem behind it. Why am I so invested in her? I should be on the hunt for Nyx. Saying goodbye to this town. Returning to business. Not letting Death find new ways to kick my arse.

"Listen, I could really do with a cup of coffee, but I have no idea what I'm supposed to order. Do you think you can help me out?"

I know, it's half ruse, and certainly not a lie, but I need this to continue. For some absurd reason that I cannot figure out, I just can't walk away from her yet. There's so much more to learn, curiosities that need feeding. Why. Do. I. Care.

Urgh.

"Okay," she says, standing, "but first I want a name."

I give her my best cocky grin, seeing I'm beginning to win her over. Oh yeah, I've still got it, baby. "Shade StormIron, at your service."

"Not yet, mister. My soul's not up for grabs for a hell of a lot more decades yet. I plan on living a very full, long life."

I try not to laugh at her expense, but she's just too damn adorable. Fuck me. As if I'd take her beautiful soul before it's due. What kind of a monster would that make me?

There's something about her that's so alluring, it effervesces from her skin like a permanent glow that calls to me. I don't know if she's doing it on purpose. I have yet to figure out what creature she is. But I know she isn't human; she has this otherworldly scent about her that all supernaturals carry.

This time we enter the coffee shop together, and she orders two cappuccinos, for which I pay. As a reaper, I have no need for money. What I do under Death's rule is my purpose—not necessarily a job, but I still earn a currency. It just happens to adapt to wherever I'm based. Luckily, the princess's tattoo allowed for that, and here I am in a town, loaded with money I'm sure several would be desperate to grab. Too bad for them I'm not a big spender, flashing my worth. No one will ever know.

"Okay, tell me. How good is this?" Thalia stares at me over the top of her large mug, lips pursed in the frothy milk.

I lift my own mug, ignoring the stares of the nosy patrons nearby; our earlier display clearly hasn't been forgotten. Don't these buggers have anything more exciting to be doing?

I take a mouthful, and hot, burning liquid coats my tongue and makes its way along my esophagus, leaving a trail in its wake. My insides have never felt so on fire before.

"You do understand the term 'hot' right?" There she goes, giving me that *you're stupid* look again. "If you still don't like it, then there's something wrong with you. Coffee is the best." Tahlia's face disappears behind her large mug, dainty fingers grasping either side of the hot drink.

Against my better judgment, I try again. This time it doesn't taste as bad, but I'm still not understanding why these earthlings have an undying lust for it. "How long have you lived here?"

Thalia glances upwards, as if the answers she seeks are printed on the ceiling. "A good few years, long enough to be calling this place home. And you? Here to stay?"

"I'm only here for work. Reapers don't normally hang around one place for long. There's always a soul calling for transport."

Her smile disappears, and sadness creeps into her face again. "That's a pity. Don't you ever want to stay in one place for more than five minutes?"

I ponder. "I've never really thought about it before. I guess I've had no reason to." I don't want to think too much about this. I fear there's a black hole at the end of a realization, if I were to have it. "What's it like working at the club?"

I pick my mug up again, forgetting that I really don't want to be drinking it. This is one human experience I'd like to take back.

Thalia quiets, a blush creeping across her cheeks. "I enjoy dancing and singing. It's the only time I feel free, confident. The music helps, I think, almost like it lulls me into a trance."

Now that I have her finally talking with passion, I don't want to interrupt with the drone of my voice, but there's so much more I want to learn.

"Don't you feel free now?" It's a strange thought that singing and dancing in public with very little, if nothing, on in the form of clothes makes her more relaxed than sitting in a coffee shop during the day, all covered up. Or is it the ogling men that give her a boost of confidence at night?

She shakes her head, her shoulders bunch up around her ears, and her hands curl around the mug she pulls into her. It's as though she's trying to make herself as small as possible, perhaps even invisible. All I want to do is take her in my arms and keep the hurt away. This Thalia is a polar opposite to the one I met last night. I can only imagine how exhausting this must be for her, but why? Why is she putting herself through this?

"There's rules in the club. Laws everyone has to abide by if they want to stay and have a good night. Melaina's good to us. One rule broken and you're banned for life. But out here, in the everyday of life, there are no protective hotheads to keep the inappropriate and despicable away. There's only me, and in comparison to many, I'm not the strong type."

A heaviness settles all around me like a black, thunderous cloud. "Do you get accosted a lot? Is that what has you pulling back from life?"

I can see it clearly. She works nights surrounded by hellhounds for protection, sleeps for most of the day, and only leaves the confines of her house when it's necessary. This isn't healthy for her, and it makes me so goddamn angry, I have to internalize my rage. If only I can get hold of the culprits behind her pain, latch onto their souls and repay in kind. It's the minimum they deserve.

She puts her empty mug back on the table, and I can feel our time together is coming to an end. I can feel her withdrawing.

"Let's just say there are a lot of people in this world who find a forest nymph's attributes highly appealing in their line of work. I can get them what they want just by the way I look. It makes me superficial. A means to an end. I am not a person, someone with life and choices. No, I am an object to be used until the magic wears off."

I see it now, the real pain behind her eyes. It's buried deep, hidden beneath doors she's erected to protect herself, one day at a time. There's loneliness in her too, and I can understand why. She won't allow anyone to get close enough because she believes there's only one thing she can offer them, the only thing they'd want from her.

Her nymph abilities.

"I don't believe that. I'm certain there are others out there who are desperate to be in your world because they want you there, not because of something you can give them."

Thalia briefly, faintly smiles, as if entertaining the notion for a moment. The instant the smile is gone, it's like she's pinged back to her reality, the world she's been living in for too long. How can I make this better? I can't just walk away. Her soul is too kind to be treated so badly.

"Tell me, Shade. Why are you even bothered about me? It wasn't my personality that drew you to me last night, was it?" She snorts, clearly becoming defensive.

I shake my head. I won't be giving her the satisfaction of thinking she's right. She's heading into a downward spiral, lashing out because I dare to think the one size shoe doesn't fit all. "It wasn't your beauty, either, Thalia. It was your song."

She rolls her eyes. "Please. I wasn't even singing last night."

"That's right. It wasn't your voice belting out the music. It was every aspect of you. You shouldn't be so quick to shut people down. They might surprise you."

"Oh yeah?" She raises a brow, crossing her arms over her chest like an overly dramatic child. "Then why don't you tell me about your past, then, Shade? How does a reaper spend his centuries?"

I fail to answer, mouth agape. I think back to the last two hundred years, and all I see is a playback of reapings, day and night, forever on the death train.

"Don't tell me how to live my life, Shade, when you haven't even experienced anything. At least I have a past, no matter how awful the memories!" She storms out of the coffee shop once more, and a strong chill passes over me.

Thalia is right to be mad, but I only want to help—to help her understand it's the restrictions she's placed on herself that are keeping her from being free. But her attack on my past, or lack thereof, is hard to digest.

I need a strong drink.

CHAPTER 9

LIVING

"*Another* of your finest, please. Just keep them coming."

The barkeep grunts at me, I'm sure because he thinks I'm being sarcastic. The Dirty Knuckle doesn't exactly sound like fine dining does it? But who am I to know any different? I'm not exactly well-educated on these kinds of experiences, as Thalia rightly, though venomously, pointed out.

"It's not like it's my fault!" I spit out between gulps of whatever beer I've been chucking down my neck all afternoon and now evening. At this point, I'm mostly talking to the air, letting out anger with bursts of conversation I've been having with myself. Replaying my coffee date with Thalia.

Everyone in here seems to keep giving me a wide berth. I don't know why. It's not like I'm crazy, just finally taking on board what I need to experience in this meat suit. Princess WitchHound gave me a gift. Why shouldn't I use it?

Clunky music blares through the bar, but nobody is dancing. I can't have that. I bring my beer with me and stomp my foot to the beat in the center of the empty floor space, sloshing more liquid on my boots than in my gullet. What a fucking waste.

I think back to the days and nights I was on a reaping hunt, and how I'd watched the people make fools of themselves on the dance floor. I try to specifically remember what they were doing with their bodies in an effort to emulate it.

I have no bloody idea how to dance, but I can't let that stop me. Fuck it. I've been a skeleton long enough. I can do the sodding robot. Move it, bitches. I got some joints to pop.

I look at my glass. It's empty of beer. How did this happen?

Oh well, time for more. Maybe I'll try this whiskey I've been hearing so much about next.

∿

"Urgh, must you really, Madame Luiza? I beg you, close the curtains, please."

"Don't you think you ought to be getting up, young man? There's no time for pity parties in this world. I didn't take you for being so weak."

I know she's trying to rile me up, but I really don't give a shit. My head pounds, and darkness is my only friend. I need sleep, not a nosy ghost nanny.

"Shade StormIron, there are souls out there that need returning to the Infernum. Now get your ass out of bed, or so help me, I will scream at the top of my lungs until you do. And trust me, I have no need for breath."

I applaud her efforts, but they're falling flat. I'm in a funk that not even the dead can bring me out of. "Go away. I'm busy being a human."

∿

I check myself in the full-length mirror, admiring the look I've got going on. Dark blue jeans. Tan Timberland boots. Tight-fitting navy tee. Black leather jacket. And the pièce de résistance? My wonderfully styled short hair.

Ladies and gentlemen, please welcome your favorite reaper in town, handsome and available, Shade StormIron!

I look at the empty bottle on the nightstand, comforted by the numbing sensation making its way into my bloodstream. It's time to get some more.

Who needs a past anyway? And so what if mine looks like a spin cycle stuck on repeat? There's nothing wrong with routine. It's dependable.

"What'cha doin', fellas? Didn't your mother tell you smoking gets you killed?" I burst out into laughter at the irony of such a notion. I'm neither alive nor dead. What the fuck is it gonna do to me? "Here, let me take these off your hands. You're far too young to have me come collecting your soul."

The few teenage kids glance at me like I'm an alien. Either that, or I've got a massive bulbous zit in the center of my forehead. Ha! Something these kids and I would have in common—greasy skin and smoke is quite the pimple attractor.

"Dude, you can't just—"

"Sure I can. Watch me. You're not even old enough for these anyway. Trust me, I'm doing you a favor."

I glare at the lit cigarette in my hand, the blurry focus making it a little challenging. "Come show grandpa how to do this. Which end am I sucking on?"

"Later, loser." The group disappear, tutting and slurring crap I care not to think about.

I take a puff, hopeful I got the right end. My tongue is still recovering from that stupid coffee. Smoke fills my mouth and instantly dries it out. I cough, and cough, and cough. Fuck me, I thought the taste is supposed to be magnificent? Why else would these humans inhale such crap? It's bloody disgusting.

I want to throw up.

My tongue is dry. Between that and the tiny blisters I've got going on, I may as well be a cat, it's so rough. Who's gonna kiss me now? I'm like sandpaper.

I try again. I must have done it wrong the first time. I hear it's something you're supposed to get used to, and with practice the technique perfects itself, right?

Right?

I touch the papery end to my lips, and that sensation alone makes my skin crawl with goose bumps. Okay, Shade. You're a badass reaper. You play with Death every day. You can inhale some dirty toxins, and not react like a sodding wimp.

Man up, loser.

I breathe it in, thankful for the blanket of night not making me so obvious. "Yup . . . No . . . Fuuuccckkkk." I cough and splutter like a choking idiot, the need for clean air highly apparent.

What the hell is wrong with people?

First coffee. Now cigarettes. So far, the only thing I can get on board with is the alcohol. Which is what I'm going to be sticking to now. I know the Dirty Knuckle is around here somewhere . . .

"SHIT, yeah, that feels good. Take it all in, babe." I watch the dark-skinned beauty wrap her plump lips around my cock, sliding down my hard shaft. She's sucking and making yummy noises, but all I can concentrate on is the fucking pleasure it's giving me.

Now this is what earthlings should be doing every damn minute of every bloody day.

Her tongue swirls around my balls, and I lose all sense. The sensation is overwhelming. It takes everything I have not to blow my load right now. I think of dead bodies, of maggots and flies feeding on carcasses.

It's no good. It's too bloody amazing to hold back. I grunt and groan, feeling an explosion welling up from the pit of my stomach.

I breathe rapidly. Short, sharp bursts of air are all I'm capable of as I lose myself and come all over her face without warning. Warm, white liquid squirts out of my dick with pride and panache like a fairy elephant making its debut show.

For some reason my black beauty isn't so pleased. She stands in all her clothes, eyes half closed with my cum all over her, arms poised on her hips. She wants to shout at me, I know, but the second she pries those plump lips apart she'll be swallowing more of me. Something I'm assuming she doesn't want to do.

"This isn't a hostel, young lady. I suggest you clean up and go."

Black beauty gasps with shock at my unwelcome guest before choking on the semen sliding into her mouth. She disappears out of my room like a bolt of lightning. One flash and she's gone.

"Great timing, Madame Luiza. You saved me a lot of effort." I grab a towel and clean up my cock, ready for round two.

"When is this nonsense going to end, Shade?"

I shrug. "I don't see one. I'm here to experience everything a human does. I already have a lifetime to catch up on, if not two. Look what I've been missing out on all this time." I point to my flesh flute. Christ, that girl made it sing.

Madame Luiza guffaws, appearing even whiter. I chuckle to myself. I never knew that was a possibility.

"Shade StormIron, you're making a fool of yourself! And what for? Some little tart in town upsets you, and now you're acting like a sullen teenager. Grow up and move on. You're not even here for this. Why do you care so much what she thinks?"

White-hot anger bubbles inside me at the suggestion of Thalia being called such a slur. Not after what I learned. To be a forest nymph in this world, a creature whose powers lie in their beauty, *surely* makes you a promiscuous being. Because looks that perfect never go untouched . . .

Please. Are people really this shallow?

"Don't talk about her like that. You don't even know." The words are forced through clenched teeth, fists bunched at my side.

"Get back to your work, and I won't." She crosses her arms over her chest, hovering above me as if the elevated height gives her some kind of supreme power over me.

She thinks she has me checkmated, but I still have another move up my sleeve.

"See you later, pain. Don't miss me too much!" I shut the door behind me, walking out of the inn before she has time to manifest downstairs and berate me some more.

If there's one thing I've learned from tonight's experience, it's that nanny ghosts don't make good wingmen.

"COME ON, just another one. It tastes sooo good."

I like this whiskey burn in my chest; it's like a constant fire keeping me warm. Not like the hollow nothing I'm accustomed to.

"Don't stop the party now," I whine, like a little girl not getting her way. I give the barman my best puppy eyes, pouting my lip too. Hey, it works with those rich kids splashed on magazines, so why not me?

I'm just as cute and adorable as the Carwashians. My butt might be letting me down, though. It's just not big and juicy like theirs.

Sigh.

"Man, I'm thirsty. Won't you help a wanderer out?"

"Looks to me like you've had enough. Don't you agree with me, Crusher?"

I turn to see the two big, burly guys standing with arms crossed over their leather cuts. Bloody hellhounds. I just can't get rid of the buggers.

"Looks like he's ready to kiss the ground, Savage. Let's say we help him?"

I shake my head, laughing wildly at this comedic duo. "Man, you guys are hilarious. Crusher and Savage, huh? Are you guys in a rock band or something?" I chortle again, imagining their bulky frames with microphones swamped by big hands, and voices so high pitched, I wonder if their balls will ever drop. "Savage, Savage . . . Where else have I heard that name?"

I'm frowning in concentration. I can feel my forehead wrinkle. Why does the name sound so familiar? Neither one wants to answer me. They've got this stoic silence going on.

"Oh, shit, yeah. You banging that HellBitch in the club?"

Savage growls, and Crusher beams as he explains, "Well, shit, man. You dead now. Melaina's his sister."

"I know." I grin. "But we both know what hellhounds are like when you're on a rampage. You'll fuck anything in sight, you horny devils."

"What the fuck did you just say to me, pretty boy?" Savage comes up close, gripping either side of my zipped jacket. His face is right up in mine, like he wants to give me a kiss.

"Wanna dance?" I raise my brows suggestively. He replies with a fist in my gut, and I immediately bend over like a prostitute.

The bar awakens with a roar, the locals yelling profanities at me like it's all my fault. But it's okay. I know they're just biased toward the hellhounds who permanently live here. Probably out of fear than loyalty.

"Outside," I hear the barkeep grunt. Crusher nods at him. Aw, it's like love at first sight, communicating with a single look.

Bleurgh.

"Come on, fellas. Why don't you just pick your panties up off the floor and we can get back to drinking?"

"Fuck you."

"After another drink, perhaps. I'm up for new experiences." I wink, and this time I anticipate his fist coming toward my face, so I block with my left and thump with my right. Bony flesh hits muscular cheek, and like a ripple effect, his skin does a mini Mexican wave.

I burst into fits of giggles—the scene keeps replaying on slow-mo in my mind.

Sadly, Savage and Crusher can't see the funnier side of this. Like two big bullies, they push me through the bar doors, and I land on my arse, head bouncing off the snowy ground like a quick-trick gymnast.

Look at me, no hands!

"What's your problem, reaper? Don't you have work to be done?"

I roll my eyes at the pair of them. "Fuck, what is it with everyone in this town and their interest in my fucking work? You never seen a reaper before? Wanna see my magic wand?"

They growl at me again. Honestly, what am I doing wrong? I offer a drink, a dance. All the things that are supposed to come before me. Ooh la la.

I stand, brushing the icy cold snow off my arse before it has any more time to seep through my boxers. Can't have a cold pickle.

"Stay down, reaper." Crusher kicks and sweeps my legs from under me, and I go down like a hooker, all business and no grace.

Darting pain shoots through my back, ripping insides I've never had to consider before.

"And keep your distance from my sister, or this won't be our only *dance*, pretty boy." Savage's fist comes down before I can even move, pain slowing everything this meat suit is capable of. It's the last thing I see—his meaty hand coming for my perfect nose, followed by spots of darkness.

CHAPTER 10

TROUBLE

*E*verything hurts.

I can't really explain it more than that. It's just a long list of body parts that have certainly seen better days. The ground is sodding freezing, and beneath me the snow has been melting long enough that I'm all shriveled up like a prune on one side of my body. I can do a one-man act of the aging process. My right side is young. My left is old.

Yet, somehow, I just can't seem to care. I've hit rock bottom—at least, I think that's what this is.

"Shade? What are you doing?"

I'm dreaming, I'm dreaming, I'm dreaming. Don't wake up. Don't wake up. Don't wake up.

I groan as she touches my shoulder, piercing through all fantasies I have that this isn't real.

"Are you okay?" Her hand disappears quickly, and like a jerk, I remember all too late how difficult it must've been for her to reach out. It makes me feel like an absolute arsehole.

"Never better," I groan, struggling to move out of the slump my sorry arse landed in last night. I don't even want to think about how long I've been out here. The fact the sky is lightening, and Thalia's standing by my feet all glammed up like she's just finished her shift at the club, tells me more than I need to know.

What is wrong with me?

Why did I let myself get in this state?

Who am I impressing like this?

I am a bloody mess, and my head pounds so hard I'm ready to throw up food I haven't even eaten.

"I guess I'll leave you to it then." Thalia turns, and I see her feet walking away from me. Did I miss something?

"Wait, please," I call, struggling to gain breath large enough to help me on my feet. "Fuck, this is embarrassing."

"Trust me, I've seen plenty of mornings people wish they weren't awake for. The night before always seems like such a good idea. You're no different."

I can't help but bristle at that. I don't know why it bothers me so much, but I don't want her to see me as another average Joe. I want to be *different* for her.

She shouldn't be seeing me like this. What the hell is wrong with me?

I get to my feet, and everything spins. I'm like a drama queen in need of rescue. I'm pathetic. Even worse, this sorry state neglected the most important aspect of his purpose.

I've let the damned souls roam free, causing chaos and carnage I can only imagine.

How can Thalia even look at me right now?

I'm disgusted with myself. Look at me, acting out like an adolescent. Madame Luiza's admonishments were spot on.

"You need help getting back to your place?"

Shit, can this get any more depressing? "It's fine. I can hobble back to the inn. I just need the world to stop spinning for five minutes first. You should go home, get out of the cold air. You're probably exhausted after a long night working."

"Do you always behave like a martyr?" She crosses her arms over her chest, looking down on me with disdain. "Shit happens to all of us, but yours is self-inflicted. Maybe if you did your job, the rest of us wouldn't have to pick up the slack. Some company isn't worth keeping."

"I'm not a martyr." I pout like a big fat baby, and I know it. I'm not after sympathy. Shit, it's the last thing I want from her right now. "Why does my job affect you?"

I raise a brow; she has me curious. What can a nymph do with souls?

"It doesn't matter. If you don't want my help, then I'll go. There's plenty of sleep for me to catch up on." She slinks away, heels disappearing into the snow without a second glance backwards.

Why do I have a feeling something terrible has happened since I've been acting out? How much have I ignored in my drunken state?

I need to drag my stupid arse to bed and start fresh. That's the sensible thing to do, but I'm not so sure I have the ability to follow logic right now. Ideally, I want to chase Thalia down. Live in some fantasy bubble where everything is right and I'm not a reaper, and we can live some happily ever after, even for five minutes. I don't want this life anymore.

Is it even life?

These messed up human emotions are ruining everything. Is this what Princess WitchHound had in mind when she cursed my tattoo this way? Does she see my torment, taking pleasure from afar?

I'm not sure what I'm good for anymore. I just know with absolute certainty that I'm disgusted with myself for even succumbing to such lowly temptations. And why? Because some girl hurt my feelings? Feelings I don't even possess when I'm out of this bloody town!

Fuck me, I'm a little sissy.

I try to get my bearings, but with the spins upsetting my vision, it's more difficult than I care to admit. I think I'm close. At least, I'm hoping this is Main Street.

Urgh.

Christ, it's freezing today. Of course, it has nothing to do with the fact I've been passed out in the snow for hours.

I think I've finally hit the highest achievement level of being human. Mission accomplished. And am I glad I'm doing the walk of shame before anyone else is awake and able to witness my finest moments.

Except the world isn't really kind enough for that, is it?

I take in a deep breath, forcing my eyesight to keep steady. I hear a faint whimper followed by a gurgling that's unmistakable.

I have nowhere near enough physical and mental stability to deal with this now. I'm more likely to capture myself than her, but the time for excuses is over. I have to act now if I'm going to save a life. Which, oddly enough, isn't really the business I'm in.

"Didn't your mother ever tell you that playing with your food is bad for you?" Thankfully there's a handy concrete pillar I can lean against for a bit more stability. It really helps me come across all powerful and in control.

The vampire-demon hybrid glares at me through black eyes with only a hint of red. Her mouth hovers above the creamy white skin of her poor prey, bright red blood trickling from the open wounds made by fangs.

"Well, at last you found me." Nyx smiles widely, blood dripping from her mouth, coating her chin. "What took you so long, Shade?"

The girl stuck in Nyx's tight grasp whispers a plea for help. She looks like she's only in her late teens, someone who hasn't even tasted the adult life yet. It's no wonder her face is pale with fear—and blood loss of course. But I know Nyx. One acknowledgment of the girl from me, and Nyx will snap her neck whether she's finished eating or not. The bitch is that sadistic.

"Please, Nyx. I haven't even tried looking for you yet—you're not so high on my priority list these days." I shrug, realizing all too late that goading her isn't the best idea when she's holding an innocent's life in her hands. Stupid, slow brain. What a time for a hangover.

"Doesn't matter anyway, you're not going to get me. I have an Underworld to get back to and rule."

I snigger, as if she could pull that off. A woman running the Underworld? Everyone knows only the men dominate the throne down below; it's just the way it is. I try to move closer, to get the girl out of Nyx's tight vise, but the creature's too busy watching my every twitch to enable me much progress. "This is why you wanted out of the Infernum? To rule another dark, depressing place?"

She shakes her head of platinum blond hair. "Oh, you're too young to understand. There's so much more you need to learn of the worlds you frequent."

I know she's just busting my balls, but I can't help but think there's a layer of truth in what she's saying. She is, after all, eight hundred years older than my two hundred. "Then why don't you explain it to me? I've got some free time on my hands."

"And let my food spoil in the meantime? Nah, I don't think so." Her head lowers to the girl's neck, and I can't move fast enough. I can't even shift forms. It's like my inebriated and hungover state has dampened everything in me, and I'm a lazy toad.

"Don't do this, Nyx. The worse you behave out here, the more you'll endure back in the Infernum. Is that what you really want?" I inch forward, keeping an eye on the girl. She doesn't look good; if anything, she's on the brink of death. I can feel it, the subtle tingles on my spine as a soul's about to become available.

Nyx cackles, but her grip never loosens on the girl—I can see it suffocating her. "What makes you think I'm going back to the Infernum? You don't honestly believe you're going to capture me, do you? I mean, look at us. We've been doing this little chit-chat for how long now? And not once have you tried to save this girl and send me back." She pauses, raising perfectly shaped brows. "Want to know what I think? You've become impotent. Performance anxiety getting you down, Shade?"

I charge, rushing for the cocky bitch who thinks she's better than everyone else. I slam into her, the weight of my body knocking her off balance. The girl gets tossed aside—not my finest moment, but at least she's somewhat safer now.

I slam my fist into the vampire-demon, catching the side of her face as she turns. She's back up on her feet before I have time to fart, let alone move. "Nyx, you're only prolonging your pain. Give up already."

I finally have enough energy to stand, but I'm still wobbly on my feet. Though, to be fair, I couldn't stand still before anyway.

Fuck, I'm weak, and I hate it. Big baby.

"Actually, Shade, I think you're just trying to delay me so you can get your own shit together. Well, unfortunately for you, I'm not a giving person." She knocks me onto my back before I even see her coming, supernatural speed on her side.

"You know, Nyx, if circumstances were different between us," I raise my brows suggestively, lifting my hips up where she's straddling me. "We could really get kinky, especially with this outfit." I run my hands over her leather-covered legs. She dresses like a dominatrix—all black leather and heels. It's a shame I know the personality beneath the clothes.

"Please. You don't know how to satisfy me." She sinks her fangs into the crook of my neck, hands pinning mine to the ground, her feet doing the same to my legs. It's like some crazy wrestling move I can't get out of.

"Ooh, this is intimate," I joke. She sinks her fangs even deeper, and I struggle not to cry out. I won't let her know how much it actually hurts—it fucking kills. There's nothing like having a gaping hole in your neck and the life sucked out of you.

"Sh-Shade?" Thalia's voice interrupts my inner monologue, and I wonder if I'm hallucinating, wishing it were her on top of me. Ooh, bad time to display my pocket rocket.

"Get off him, you crazy bitch!" Thalia yells, and this time I know it's real.

Nyx is lifted off my body, and with a lot of effort, I'm back on my feet, blood dripping from my neck in a steady trickle. Is that good or bad? Better than a gush, right?

"Well, well, well. What do we have here? Shade's gone and gotten himself a playmate. You're a pretty thing."

I wobble over to Thalia, shielding her with my own beat-up body. What's a little more pummeling gonna do? Kill me? I'd like to see what happens then.

"You stay away from her. She's not your concern. Besides, she doesn't suit your tastes. Too much super in her natural."

I glance around, looking for the human. She's barely holding on to breath. Frankly, I'm amazed she's lasted this long. I admire her fighting to live.

I feel Thalia move behind me, coming to stand at my side. A silent conversation passes between the two females in a mighty staredown. I have no bloody idea what's going on, but Nyx is backing up. What the hell is a vampire-demon afraid of a nymph for? It's not like Thalia has any kind of advantage over Nyx—at least, not one I know of. Thalia's powers lie in beauty, not strength.

"Catch you later, Shade. I'll be back for that kiss, beautiful." Nyx winks at Thalia, and I'm thrown. I've been bashed around upside the head, which is why I'm confused. It has to be, right? Doesn't make sense otherwise. The pair don't know each other, do they? Fuck me, have I fallen for the one creature whose sexual orientation lies in women too? This can be interesting. Now how do I go about asking for a threesome? Is there some kind of manual for this stuff?

"Come on, we need to get you cleaned up. Her, too." Thalia comments on the girl groaning on the ground. How she hasn't frozen to death I'll never know.

"What did you do to Nyx, Thalia?" I'm amazed. There's no other word for it. Nyx has disappeared *and* left her snack behind. This shit never happens.

Thalia shrugs, as if it were nothing. "You saw, nothing special. Come on, she needs a doctor. Are you going to help me?"

"What's going on here?"

What is it with people popping up out of nowhere in this town? Don't they have the courtesy to at least cough to announce their presence?

"Sheriff, we need to get to the medical center. She's been attacked." Thalia kneels down by the girl. Judging by everyone's faces, no one knows her name.

"Is this your doing?" The sheriff frowns at me, fists bunched at his sides as if he's getting ready to tackle me. It's a bad day to be Shade—I've kissed more floors than females.

"No, it's the creature I'm hunting. Thalia can vouch for me." I glance at the beautiful nymph who's too concerned with the girl to be listening to what I have to say. Great.

"Don't even think about leaving town. I'll be back for questions." The sheriff lifts the girl and takes her to his car. A scent of wolf shifter hangs in the air.

I couldn't be more ashamed of myself if I tried. My stupidity put this girl's life in danger. I hope there haven't been more.

"Come on, Shade. Let's stitch you up." Thalia turns, heading in the direction she'd been walking before my drama caught up with her.

I follow, curious to see where she's taking me. I catch up, feet slushing in a mix of day-old snow and fresh powder. The town is still quiet—it takes on its own enchantment with all the Christmas decorations.

"How was work?" I ask, genuinely interested in her day, or more precisely, night.

"Busy, as always. I've been working on a new routine, but I just can't nail this one move that ties the whole sequence together. It's driving me insane." She grunts, rifling through the bag dangling off her shoulder. She produces a set of keys as we near a row of houses, and pauses a few moments as we reach a green door. Is she afraid of inviting me in? Having second thoughts about her actions?

I don't want to make her feel uncomfortable in her own home. It isn't right.

"Thalia, I can go . . ."

She slips the key in the lock, turns, and smiles my way. "Don't be silly. We're here now. We just need to sort this wound before you get an infection."

I want to laugh, but I think better of it. Knowing my luck, this meat suit *would* contract an infection just to dampen my progress with soul-snatching even more.

Stepping into the hallway, I take note of all the homey decorations she has. Paintings of beautiful landscapes hang on the walls, comforting pillows and blankets are draped on the sofa in the main room, and candle holders and vases of flowers cover every surface available. Strangely, even amongst the warmth this home brings, there's also an ominous chill in the considerable lack of pictures. There are no frames containing photos of family members, friends, even places she's visited. It's cold, as though the house is projecting the loneliness within Thalia.

"The bathroom is through there. I'd rather not get blood on the carpets in the living room." Thalia half smiles as though apologizing. "I'll just go get the bandages."

I tell myself not to follow her, willing my feet to walk toward the bathroom instead, and wait diligently like a good boy.

"Does it hurt?" Thalia catches me off guard, walking into the bathroom while I have my eyes closed.

"A little, not as much as before." I try shaking it off—can't have this gorgeous lady thinking I'm any less than the man she deserves. Christ, I want to be that guy.

"This is all new for you, huh? The coffee, the alcohol, the fights?" She raises a brow at my black eye, wetting a cotton ball before placing it on my neck to clear the blood away.

"I've never been made to feel like a human before. It's . . . different than what I assumed. Lots of emotional baggage," I sum up.

She sighs, frowning hard, pulling what looks like crossed tape off its sticky backing and putting the butterfly-like stitches on my neck, no needle necessary.

"Trust me, I know all about emotional turmoil. It's why I don't . . . Why I can't . . ." She pauses longer this time, struggling to voice what's churning in her mind. "Relationships are messy even before being accused of manipulating thoughts, making someone fall in love with you against their will."

Her eyes bore into mine, and her hands disappear from my neck. Her lips are inches from mine, and it takes every kind of patience I've ever learned to keep from closing the gap and kissing her. This has to be on her terms. I won't make her feel pressured.

"I can't really comment. I've never experienced it before."

She pulls back, eyes blinking as though clearing from a trance. "You know, you make it difficult to believe this is all new to you at times. You seem so relaxed, so at ease with who you are, despite having everything turned upside down. It makes me feel weak, makes me wish I were stronger, more capable of accepting the world as it is, instead of hiding from it."

I swallow hard. "I can help you, Thalia. Let me in, and I'll prove you have a fierce confidence within you that's desperate to be unleashed."

She slips a plaster over her handiwork on my neck, and clears everything away without saying a word. As though needing the time to digest what I've offered. It pains me she doesn't immediately agree. That she even has to think about it shows me how much she shelters herself away from life unless it revolves around dancing at the club.

This makes me sad. She's so much more than this.

"I'll see myself out," I say, realizing she isn't going to answer me, and I've made things too awkward to stay any longer.

Just as I reach the front door, I hear her small voice. "Shade, I'm not a quick fix. I won't be magically healed by morning. You won't even be here long enough to help me back on my feet the way you think I need to be."

I close the gap between us in the hallway, doing my best not to reach out and touch her. "Thalia, I don't think you're broken. You just haven't unlocked your full potential yet. I'm not even suggesting I'm the right person to do that for you either, but I'm selfish enough to tell you I want to. Spending time with you unlocks new experiences within me. I don't want to give that up yet either."

I step back toward the front door again, knowing we both need space. I open the door and step outside, holding the handle to close it behind me. "Think about it, Thalia. I already see your beautiful soul."

CHAPTER 11

BUSINESS

"Feeling better now?"

I hang my head in shame before Madame Luiza as she hovers in her favorite spot at the foot of the bed. The bed covers just about hide my drumstick, not that she hasn't seen it before, but I'm on a new road of redemption. I can't be making her blush at my wanger. It's ungentlemanly of me.

"How big of an apology do I owe you?"

"Why don't you get those pesky souls back where they belong, and we'll call it even? It's nice to see you've got your head on straight again."

I cower under the covers, feeling like a scorned boy. "I don't know what to say. Have you heard anything about the girl from yesterday?"

Madame Luiza shakes her head, moving closer to the side of the bed and perching on the edge as though she truly were sitting there. "Sheriff Kasun dropped by, gave Michaela quite the aggravation. You're lucky he didn't storm in here and wake you up himself."

Add another on my very long list of reasons to be thankful for Whisper Falls Inn and its owner.

"Is the girl still alive, did he say?"

"Yes, dear. She's holding on after a blood transfusion. Oddest thing is we still don't know where she's from. I imagine that's what the sheriff wants to know, that and how she ended up with a gaping hole in her neck, of course."

I rub my hands over my face. "I'm going to have a lot to answer for." I sigh loudly. "What about Nyx? Any gossip surrounding her whereabouts that could help me?"

"Now then, Shade. I thought you reapers were able to feel a soul when it's near. Are you suggesting you can't feel hers lurking around?"

I shake my head. "I don't know why, but I'm not the only one. Princess WitchHound hasn't said anything about the vampire-demon running around town, and she was quick to jump on my arse the second I landed in this town."

Madame Luiza frowns. "Princess WitchHound?"

"You know, light brown hair, covered in tattoos, stone in her nose, and more jewelry than body parts to wear it on?"

"You mean Adelaide? She's Michaela's best friend, I'll have you know, and a talented witch at that. You watch what you're saying, young man."

I hold up my hands. "I'm not disputing that. It just has me wondering how Nyx has gone past her detection spells and continues to fly under the radar of mine, too. It makes zero sense."

Madame Luiza seems to take what I'm saying on board, if the fierce concentration on her ghostly appearance is anything to go by. "Perhaps she has some magic working of her own. Is she known for it?"

I shake my head. "She doesn't possess those skills. The only way she'd get magic is through force or blackmailing someone who can. You know the people in this town better than I do. Hell, all I seem capable of doing is making enemies and pissing everyone off. Do you think there's anyone here that would bow down to Nyx?"

She huffs. "That's a loaded question, Shade. We all have a weakness to exploit—all it takes is the right reward."

I think it through. "Who has the most to gain? Fuck, she's a crafty bitch." I get out of the bed, needing to stretch my legs and pace the small length of the room. It's better than nothing. "So besides scorning my inability to feel her, do you have anything else that can help me?"

Madame Luiza shrugs, a cheeky smile gracing her face. "It's amazing what can be heard when you're able to walk through walls, and my oh my, do these ones talk." She winks, clearly proud of herself.

"Okay, I see what's going on here. What's it going to cost me for this information?"

"You make it sound so dirty, Shade. I'm a lady. I wouldn't infer tit for tat, you know. But if a ghost ever happens to change her mind, I want a promise and assurance that you'll be there to guide her on to the next stage."

"You have my word, Madame Luiza. Just call my name, and I'll hear your soul sing. I promise it will be painless."

She nods, a troubled expression coloring her face. I don't know what to make of it, other than the turmoil of eventually leaving living family behind for good. I have seen its effect many times—no one is ever the same again, but time will inevitably bring them together once more. It's the decades between that are the struggle.

"I don't know when," she begins, but I cut her off.

"It doesn't matter. When you're ready, I'll be around for you. It's the least I can do, all things considered."

She gives me a half smile, and I can see I'm bringing her back out of the sadness of her deep thoughts. "If what I've heard is true, then Nyx has been hanging around that motorcycle club a lot. Ask me, I'd say she fits right in there. Trouble plays well with its own kind."

I can't help but smile at her disdain. It's the same reaction she had to Silk, the nightclub. Oddly enough, both are run by hellhounds. I wonder if she has some kind of prejudice against them. That would be something, considering she herself pointed out that her niece's best friend is part hothead. Does Auntie Luiza not approve?

"What would she get from the club?" I'm thinking out loud, but Madame Luiza answers anyway.

"What could you do with a whole club of hellhounds and shifters at your disposal?"

"Shit." I grab my clothes, making the connection. "I could kiss you right now!" I head for the door, but Madame Luiza calls out, halting my progress.

"You can't just walk into the club, Shade. There are rules."

I shake my head, smiling broadly. "I know that. Look at you worrying about me. It makes me feel all warm and gooey inside."

"Don't ruin it. What are you going to do?"

"I'm going to the next best place on the list. I hear family bonds are really strong amongst hellhounds." I wink and close the door.

CHAPTER 12

ALLIES

Fuck me, I hope she's in a good mood today. The pod starts ascending through the trees, Melaina's bodyguard watching with utter hatred at my ease of access. Ahem.

Melaina steps forward as I leave the pod, already waiting for me. "Shade, I'd say it's a pleasure, but we'd both know I'd be lying. What's up? And don't tell me there's a soul here, because I know for a fact there isn't right now. Club's empty. Only my dancers are practicing their routines."

"Actually, I came to speak to you. Do you have time?"

She narrows her eyes at me. "The fact you're asking so nicely has me on edge. I don't like it. What do you want?"

"I met your brother," I begin. She rolls her eyes and immediately turns from the main entrance, heading for her office. I must have earned her seal of approval for privacy with this conversation. Family matters clearly aren't for the nosy to hear. Interesting.

"What did Tychon do that you think I'm going to help you with?" She folds her arms over her chest, one leg crossed seductively over the other as she takes one of the armchair seats. Once again she's dressed in a figure-hugging dress that accentuates her tits, and fuck-me heels that deserve to be wrapped around a man's shoulders. Hell yeah, I bet she's an animal in bed, wild with lust.

Oops. Don't get a stiffy, don't get a stiffy, don't get a stiffy.

Think floppy.

"Nothing," I begin, then catch myself. That isn't the total truth really, is it? "Well, he gave me a couple of shiners, some broken ribs, and knocked me out cold in the freezing conditions all night, but other than that, can't complain. Yet."

"Well, I'm sure you deserved it. You have a way of pissing us off. So if it's not about getting back at him, what is it you want?"

I make myself comfortable on her couch, this time leaving my feet firmly on the carpet. I've begun to understand you don't get answers in this world without a sweetener first. And respecting Melaina's furniture is step one.

I know. I'm a sodding suck-up now.

"Do you know what goes on at SIN?"

"You do realize I don't keep tabs on my brother, right? I'm not his mother, and I'm busy enough here."

I tilt my head to the side. "Still doesn't really answer my question, though, does it? Let me be a bit more precise. Have you seen, or has your brother mentioned anything about a new arrival lately? A platinum blonde, leather-loving, vampire-demon bitch to be exact."

Melaina starts to laugh. "I didn't peg you for a motorcycle groupie fucker. What's the matter, sugar? Couldn't satisfy her needs, so she hops to the first sex orgy she can find?"

Sex orgy? Is this what happens at the motorcycle club? Sounds like I need to become a member. Immediately.

"She's not my type," I answer dryly. "But I certainly do want her. You would, too, if you knew who she was. This is one soul that belongs in the Infernum indefinitely."

Melaina leans forward, legs uncrossed as if she now means business. "What makes you think she's affiliated with my brother?"

I have to appreciate her loyalty. Not once has she slipped up and revealed information *I* need. No, she's just continually pumping me for answers instead. Clever bitch.

"That's what I'm trying to find out. Are you telling me you don't know anything, or are you just trying to delay me by covering for your brother?"

Anger is bubbling within me, close to the surface. One wrong answer and I'm going to be flipping my lid. I'm sick of wasting time. I'm sick of not knowing how to control this body and its fucking emotional roller coaster.

Melaina stares, and I glare back, neither one of us blinking.

"Shit," she murmurs, getting out of her chair. "We may have a problem closer to home. This Nyx you've described, I believe I've seen her."

I stand, not sure why, but it feels like the right thing to be doing. "Where?"

"Here. In *my* club. Tell me, what's your interest in Thalia?"

I scoff, brushing her off as being ridiculous. "I don't have an interest. Reaper, remember? We don't get to embrace fantasy-like notions."

She smiles widely. Melaina moves toward me, coming up into my face as she backs me into a corner, trapping me. "I knew it. You like her more than you want to admit. But how does this end, Shade? You break her heart and return to do Death's bidding, never to reappear."

I shake my head, having already battled with this myself every time I catch a glimpse of Thalia, and I'm reminded that the stunning image I remember doesn't do her justice. She takes my breath away more than I'll ever be able to admit. I know this makes me a coward, but I'm struggling to understand it myself. This is all new territory to me.

"Hurting her is the last thing I want to do. It's why I *haven't* pursued anything more."

"I take care of my girls, Shade. And Thalia's been through enough without you adding to her pain. Do I make myself clear?"

"You know, hellhound, I like you. You don't bullshit, and I appreciate that. It's a lost quality in this day and age." I lean forward, closing any kind of space between us. "But I'm not here for Thalia. It's Nyx I want. So why did you change the subject?"

Melaina turns away, running hands through her long, luscious locks. "Before you get all hotheaded on me, I don't know all the details. Only what I've seen."

"And that is?" I struggle to hold on to my temper. Why is she dragging this out so much?

She sighs loudly, clearly having made up her mind about something. "Nyx was here, and she took a vested interest in Thalia. I don't know what was said, but I warned Thalia to be careful. Now that you're here, I can see some dots connecting. Somehow, Nyx knows about your interest in my nymph, and I can guarantee Thalia's going to pay the price for it. What the fuck is going on, Shade?"

I shake my head, pacing to and fro. "No, that can't be. There's nothing Thalia can give Nyx that works to her advantage."

Melaina comes up to me and smacks my head.

"Hey! What was that for?" I caress my temple, now pulsing from her fleshy sting.

"Are you really this dumb? Of course Nyx has something to gain from Thalia if Thalia has feelings for you, too! Fuck, why are men so clueless when it comes to love? This isn't rocket science, Shade."

I deny her observations. There's no way. "Not once has she hinted she's interested in me. You're just blowing smoke up my arse now. Why are you being so cruel?"

"Urgh!" Melaina shoves me out of her office. "Stop being an idiot, or I *will* let my rage out on you. Don't you see what advantage Nyx has to gain in this?"

I stare blankly, which isn't the right answer if the despair on Melaina's face is anything to go by. In fact, she's so tightly wound, it's like she's constipated right now.

"Fuck me, do I have to spell it out for you? She'll use Thalia to get to you, and once she has you . . ."

I shrug. "Nyx doesn't want me taking her back to the Infernum, so she'll try to get rid of me."

This isn't really a marvelous revelation. In fact, it's bloody obvious. For the vampire-demon, I'm what stands between her and freedom to rule the Underworld. Ha! It still makes me chuckle every time I try to imagine a female on the throne. Christ, even the lowly creatures would ridicule her rule. Can't be a leader without a following.

"Why aren't you panicking about this?" Melaina frowns, hands on hips.

"Because I'm not the only reaper in Death's arsenal. If I don't get the job done, he'll send another, and another, and another until it is. You can't tell me Nyx hasn't thought of that."

"Yes, but you're her immediate threat. There's nothing more to it than that."

It can't really be that simple, can it? But how can Melaina be so sure when I haven't even explained Nyx's motive behind it all? How would she know I'm Nyx's temporary problem, standing between her and the Underworld? But then, how is she taking over the Underworld without an army behind her? This is what I was hoping to find out from Melaina. I'm sure Nyx has some dastardly plan to use SIN's club members to act on her behalf. Are they even aware of what's in store for them?

I feel so bloody clueless.

"What are you gonna do, Shade? Because I'm not losing any of my girls to this crazy soul you let escape."

"I didn't let them escape, dammit. It's not like I stood by the portal and said, 'Hey, guys, fancy a free ride back to earth to wreak some havoc?' Clearly Nyx has been planning this for a long time. And I'm the sucker that got stuck with cleanup. So before you go around pointing the finger, I'd reevaluate your own mistakes."

I make haste. This stupid back and forth conversation isn't getting me anywhere, and I'm clearly wasting precious energy on this. "Call me when you have something of use to give me," I shout, walking down the hallway, turning a corner and entering the maze of corridors that lead to rooms I have yet to explore—though that's for when I have the time.

"I don't know if I can do this," a male whisper carries through the hallway.

I stop. I'm not sure why, but I have this strange suspicion that I'm meant to listen.

"Don't even think about chickening out on me."

I freeze. The female voice is unmistakable. How long has she been here?

"You're bringing me the nymph whether you want to or not. I have your life in my hands, remember? You do what I say or your precious future in the club is gone. I don't think the president will take too kindly to a weakling such as you."

I peek around the corner wall, hoping to see who Nyx is trying to coerce, but really I'm lucky enough that she hasn't noticed me so far. Her instincts are always too perfect to sneak up on.

I take it slowly, making sure to keep my breathing even and quiet.

"When? When do you want this done?" There's an unmistakable quiver in the male's voice, but I still can't see. All I can catch a glimpse of is a leather cut. It isn't much to go on, considering I've already heard about an affiliation to the club. Proof that Nyx has been running amok there.

"When do you think, you babbling buffoon? Immediately. Get it done. I'll be waiting."

Footsteps come my way. I do the only thing I can. I turn and run away.

Fuck me. I need to save Thalia.

CHAPTER 13

DAMSELS

*S*he's mesmerizing. Not an ounce of care mars her beautiful features. She's calm, happy, enjoying the music as she dances to the upbeat tempo. It's like the first night I saw her all over again. Limbs contort around the metal pole; she's a professional gymnast with complete control over her strength. I can't imagine the hours of training it takes for such discipline.

She catches my eye, her step falters, and she misses the beat. She tries to pick it up again, but I've clearly distracted her too much. I wonder why.

"Looks like you're back to your normal self," she calls, moving to sit on the edge of the small square stage.

"Yup, I'm all healed. Turns out this meat suit likes to take on some of my reaper abilities when it wants to. Too bad it hasn't helped much before now."

"So what are you doing here? Come to give me a hard time for working at the club?"

I frown, taken aback. "Why would I do that?"

She waves her hand, as if passing it off. "Plenty of people have strong opinions about what we do here. I guess I've just been waiting for you to express yours."

"You've been getting a hard time for dancing?" I raise a brow, intrigued. Who'd dare question the use of such talent? "Want me to kick some asses?"

She laughs, a sound I've rarely heard but will do anything to bring out of her again. She's got me hooked. At this rate, she can ask me to do anything, and I'll gladly do it, no matter the price.

"Listen, I need you to come with me." I hold out my hand.

"Why? I'm working. I can't just leave."

I shake my head. How much do I tell her? Do I scare her, use fear to get her to do what I want so that I can protect her?

Honesty has always been my motto; I won't change now. "Your life is in danger, Thalia. Please, trust me."

She recoils from my touch, a reaction that stings even more every time it happens. Hadn't we gotten over this hurdle yet?

She stands, towering above me as she's on the raised platform. "Are you threatening me, Shade? Is this because I haven't given you an answer about helping me yet? You're making up trouble to get me to agree?"

Where the hell does that notion come from? "No, I'm offering you my protection, Thalia. I need to keep you safe from what's coming."

She thrusts her left hip out, hands firmly placed on her sides. "You mean you need to keep me for yourself to help you feel human or whatever? Well, no thank you. I'd rather take my chances here with the protection we've already got against this so-called danger I'm in."

I shake my head. She doesn't understand. "Why won't you trust me?" I lean on the edge of the platform, looking up in earnest. "I'm trying to save your life."

She takes the steps down from the stage, turning toward me. "You've given me no reason to trust you, Shade. If anything, you make me question things even more. I don't need your help. I've been saving myself for years, despite your assumptions about me." She walks away, heading to an area clearly designated as off-limits to non-personnel. Changing rooms, I think.

I can't force Thalia to take me up on my offer, but I also can't sit back and watch the inevitable. Nyx has someone coming for Thalia. She might not comprehend the true danger she's in, but no way in hell am I going to let them take her.

I'm no white knight, but for Thalia, I'll be the hero she deserves, one incognito move at a time. Starting with Nyx.

~

MY SPINE TINGLES, running a current from my neck to my coccyx and back again. It's an unmistakable feeling, and one I'm more than thankful for at this moment. I need a distraction. A win in the Shade box for a change.

I follow the sensation, the pin pricks increasing the closer I come. I move through the town, darkness having cloaked the sky, making the Christmas lights illuminate like colorful stars. I consider the holiday decorations for a brief moment, the town busy with late-night shoppers preparing for the big day in a few days. If I could live in this dimension, I could easily see myself being sucked into the festive spirit. The smiles and cheer are practically contagious. I've never known anything like it.

What would it be like to wake up on Christmas morning in a house fully decorated with Thalia at my side? Does she like this season? I can imagine the glow on her face as she sees the presents under the tree, her name plastered all over them. I would spoil her rotten, a small example of my growing love for her.

"Yeah, right. As if that's ever going to happen," I mumble to myself, sadness threatening to send me into a deep depression. Not now. I'm not falling back into the trap of moping around again.

I square my shoulders and get back on track, dodging shoppers left and right as the soul calls me on until I reach the place it's hiding. There's no mistaking this is it. My spine is going into meltdown mode with pain.

Havenwood Falls High.

What the hell is a soul doing at a bloody school, for god's sake? Suddenly feeling the need to get smart?

I shake my head, laughing at my own joke. Where's an audience when you need one?

The tattoo on my arm vibrates. I can feel the change coming on, allowing me to return to my natural state. Skin, muscles, blood, and organs disappear as though being ripped away from me. Oddly enough, it's painless, probably because they were never mine to begin with.

I feel my wings desperate to be stretched, begging for freedom. I flex the beauties, stretching wide until they're pulled taut. I hover above the ground, a black mist that enables me to become invisible except to the soul that's calling.

I slip through the school doors, instincts taking over as I zoom through the corridors, working my way around the building as though it's a place I've frequented many a time before.

"Well, well, well. Bingo," I call, seeing the soul in the middle of a classroom, book upon book spread across the table in front of it. "You escape torture and your ideal haven is a school? What's wrong with you?" I laugh out loud, gaining the soul's attention. It was so immersed in the textbooks, it had no idea I slipped in. This doesn't make a lick of sense.

"I like to read. What's wrong with that?"

I shake my head. "Nothing, but the last time I checked you're a monster, not a student. Are you trying to atone for your sins?"

"It's none of your business, reaper. Get out of here. You don't own me."

I tut loudly, snatching the soul tight before it has time to register my intentions. "That's where you're wrong, mate." I speed through the corridors, calling upon a portal to open up for us to slip through.

The soul struggles, trying to wrangle free from my grasp. I hold on tighter, flapping my wings faster.

"There's no other choice for you, mate. This is where you belong."

The Infernum opens up, loud screeches, roars, and yells playing out—the place's own theme song. The temperatures climb to a mighty swelter in here. I see the way it affects the creatures, wearing them down, bodies decaying in record time.

I find an empty cell along my assigned cages, this length of the Infernum reserved for my captures. The Infernum only lets them out to wander the abyss when it deems them ready. Until then, they remain bound to chains I've pinned them into. This soul is no different.

I shackle the soul and disappear, scrambling out of this place before any more mishaps can happen. I make sure the portal closes behind me, no unwanted hitchhikers trying to sneak out, and pop back into the waiting portal at the high school in this weird and wonderfully charming town.

The large bubble of opalescent energy shifts and reduces in size until finally it disappears, sealing completely. My wings fold into my spine, and I'm once more shifting forms, this evil tattoo at work already. Honestly, it's like I have to beg for it to get me out of this skin suit, but the second I'm back in this world, BAM! Instant dressing.

"You're in my town, and you've got my people in a spell. You'd better start talking, and fast, or there will be hell to pay."

What's going on? I recognize that voice, coming from one of the rooms. I take myself and my big nosy nose around the building until I find the source of the voice. It's the sheriff, with a group of people I haven't seen in a long time.

I slip into the back of the room and watch the scene unfold, trying not to get too involved. I make some quick jibes about Hell. How can I not, when they're cursing the place? Then I disappear out of the room before the sheriff has time to chase me down and question me over the girl Nyx took a healthy dose from.

Oh, sodding Nyx. What am I gonna do about her?

Holy shit. I'm in heaven.

There's no other word for the deliciousness in front of me. A juicy burger stuffed with bacon and melted cheese, a basket of fries, and a chocolate milkshake so big, it's like swimming in dessert.

I'm never leaving this place again. Screw my responsibilities. The gods of food have taken me in; I'm no longer fit for purpose.

Please?

Everything in this Burger Bar is perfect, from the appreciative and happy servers to the pretty holiday decorations that just want to banish every Grinch-like personality. Actually, the only thing that's letting this place down is its taste in music. I'm just not a fan of the Beatles. However, if Thalia managed to find a way to dance to this crap, I may just change my mind. Mostly because the music would disappear as I lose myself in her. Fuck me, I need to see her. Keeping my distance is turning me inside out. I want to shag her senseless and knock the idiocy out of her at the same time. It's a confusing time for me.

Thankfully, I at least have food to comfort me, and I'm instantly berating myself for not coming here sooner. I've been neglecting a lot of my human needs. It's not until my meat suit practically screams at me to go to the bathroom or find some sustenance that I even remember I need those things to make it through the day. I should probably get it stamped on my hand or something as a reminder.

I take a big bite out of my burger, chewing slowly to savor the experience. I want to remember this place when I'm back to my skeleton ways.

"No, no, no. Not now." I want to cry. I'm not ready to say goodbye to my food. There's a special bond between a man and his grub, and I'm just beginning to understand it, but my spine tingles again. I'm just about ready to curse these souls to hell for bloody interrupting the one good thing I've finally got going on. Couldn't it have waited just another thirty minutes?

Reluctantly, I leave the restaurant, giving my food moon eyes for the last time. I step outside, the drive-in surprisingly empty of the town's teenagers. Apparently, it's a known hotspot for the curious adolescents.

"Oh, and this will be why," I mumble to myself, coming up to my destination. It seems a large percentage of the town's population has gathered in one place. "What is this?" I see a sign with large script written in blue ink. "Cold Moon Ball." I scratch my chin. "I guess my invite got lost in the post."

I keep getting stared at, and I'm not sure if it's because I'm talking out loud to myself or because my attire doesn't correlate with the fancy pants festivities. Jeans and boots aren't welcome among the black tie suits and ball gowns parading around like kings and queens. Uppity fuckers. If only they knew I get to decide where their souls end up in the afterlife. Mwahahaha.

I pause. The call for a reaping has suddenly disappeared; the soul's been saved. Christ, I can't catch a break. This town is proving to be one big bloody nemesis! I could've finished my food after all. I am *not* happy.

"Where the fuck have you been?"

I'm stopped in my tracks by a beautiful babe demanding my attention. I'd almost consider myself lucky, except for who it is.

"Working. You? Shot any more guys through the heart with your big mama bear speeches?"

She frowns, grabbing my arm, burning my skin. "Stop being so pathetic. Is she with you?"

I shake my head, confused. "What the fuck are you talking about, Melaina? Is who with me?"

"Thalia, of course! Who else? She's not been at the club all day, and when her shift started two hours ago, she still didn't show. I thought you finally decided to sweep her off her feet and screw me over."

My eyes widen with fear. "You mean she's missing? She's not just taking a day off sick or something?"

Melaina laughs. "You're so naïve. Thalia's never taken a day off from the moment she started working for me. My girl doesn't get sick either."

I rub my hands over my face, feeling a chill run through my bones that isn't only created by the freezing temperatures.

"Nyx took her," I whisper, not wanting to admit the truth. I left her to fend for herself, sure it's what she wanted, but I shouldn't have listened. I should've done the man thing I've seen so often and forced my protection on her. This is what I get for allowing her the freedom of making choices for herself. "I'm an idiot."

"Why are you saying this? Where would Nyx take her? This has the Collector written all over it." Melaina's standing strong, hands on hips. All business. She's certainly projecting an attitude that's keeping onlookers away.

I shake my head. Again with the bloody Collector. Who is this douche? "At Silk, I overheard Nyx trying to coerce someone from SIN into taking Thalia. I tried to get Thalia to come with me then, but she insisted she had all the protection she needed. She blew me off."

"And you took her word for it? You *are* a fucking idiot. I thought *you* were taking care of her after our chat! What the fuck have you been doing?"

"I was, until she rejected me! I was pissed. It's not like I put myself out there for everyone, you know. I needed to cool off, then I got distracted with reaping. Nyx is now the last soul I need to return before I can get back to regular scheduling."

"And you didn't think that happened to be a ploy to keep you distracted, better still in another dimension? Come on, Shade. Use your head. Nyx played you, again."

I shrug. Whether she's right or not doesn't make much difference now. "It doesn't matter, Melaina. When a soul calls, I have no choice but to go to it. That's how I've been made."

"Which she exploited. You ever wonder why she wasn't the only soul that escaped that day? I bet this has been her plan all along, using the other souls to keep you distracted long enough to meet her end goal. I'm assuming she has one, besides fucking everyone else's lives up."

"She wants the Underworld, and if you're right, then I guess this means she's got her army ready to back her up. But why Thalia?"

Melaina gives me one of her famous head smacks. It makes my ears ring like Santa's sleigh bells. "To finish you off, dummy. Where would she take her?"

"You're not gonna like the answer." I sigh, my shoulders aching with tension. "There's only one place I know she's been using to hide, if my sources are right."

Melaina groans, catching on. "This is why you wanted to know about my brother and SIN, isn't it?"

"Ding, ding, ding. We have a winner."

"Fuck you, reaper."

"All in good time, baby. One damsel at a time, please."

CHAPTER 14

CHALLENGES

I snoop around the outskirts of the SIN building, grateful for the night's blanket of darkness. Parked Harleys are lined up like soldiers on parade. Under any other circumstances, I'd take a moment to appreciate the glorious machines. Fear for Thalia's life has me distracted enough. Where is she? She has to be close.

I slip into the MC, the back entrance left wide open and unoccupied. I don't like this. It smells like a trap.

"She's not here, reaper. You can stop hiding."

I walk into the main room. When did I lose my stealth? Standing in the center of the room, I see my two buddies, Savage and Crusher.

"I just got off the phone with my sister. Interesting chat. You think a vampire-demon's been sniffing around here without me knowing?"

In for a penny, in for a pound, right? I'm already in the shit by the looks of it. "What better place to get an army of rebels than here?"

Savage roars, coming toward me. It's like a repeat of that night at the bar all over again.

"Listen, I don't know for sure who she has or hasn't corrupted. I just know creatures who aren't too fussy about what side of the law they sit on appeal to her nature. And she's good at manipulating everything she wants. She's got my girl, and I'm getting her back, one way or another. You gonna help?"

Savage cracks his knuckles, glancing at Crusher. "How can you be so sure this isn't the Collector's gig?"

I grit my teeth. "I don't know who this bloody Collector is! My battle is with Nyx. I see no other logical reason for anyone else to be involved."

Savage grunts after a momentary pause. "We've got members hunting the town already. When they find Nyx, we'll know."

I shake my head. I can't stay here, being still. I have to be doing *something*. "She wouldn't take Thalia someplace open for anyone to walk in on. Not unless she wants to be found," I begin, confusing my own thoughts as I think out loud. What did Nyx do?

"Where?"

I lift my head, noticing the phone Savage has pinned to his ear. I didn't even hear it ring.

"On it." He pockets the device, striding for the door. "She's in the cemetery."

I rush ahead. "Meet you there."

I call on my reaper form, begging for my tattoo to let me roam free. Now more than ever I need my abilities at full strength.

My wings pop open, and I'm almost giddy with appreciation. I ascend to the sky in a quick burst of energy, zooming through the air until I see the cemetery below. It's taken less than twenty seconds. And in the background I hear the roar of motorcycles approaching at speed too.

I take a sweep of the grounds, surprised to find Melaina and Princess WitchHound are already here. Sneaky bitch. No wonder she didn't follow me to her brother's club; she had her own agenda.

I land on my feet beside the two of them, skelly and cape back in action. Princess doesn't seem so upset to see me like this, not like I expected.

"She's in there. Hasn't come out yet."

"Why? What is this place?" I point to the large boulder fused with trees. It doesn't look like much to me.

Princess shakes her head. "It's just an empty cave. One way in, one way out. Not quite sure what she expects to achieve here." The rock-chic beauty frowns, which has me concerned, considering the amount of power she wields.

"So, let's storm right in and get this over with, shall we?"

Behind me, I hear Savage and Crusher join us on foot, their bikes obviously parked up.

"Face it, Nyx. This is over," I yell into the cavern. I see her platinum blond hair, illuminating the way before the rest of her comes into view.

"You're right, Shade. It's finally time to get it all done with."

Overhead, a scream echoes as two females jump from the tree above. Their faces are wildly feral, fangs stood proud from their mouths, bright red eyes from the demon who sired them.

I now know the fate of Nyx's mealtime victims.

"You went back to finish her off?" I point to the girl on the right, the teenager who I thought was safe in the hospital.

Nyx laughs, clearly happy. "Why wouldn't I? They're not the only ones either." She winks, and suddenly the cemetery is filled with an army of poor, helpless victims who know no better than the savageness of their first month as vampire-demons. "Aren't you going to congratulate me, Shade? I have a big family."

They all come, crowding around us all at once, blocking us into a tight circle.

"Any brilliant plans, Shade?" Melaina asks, stance ready to fight.

"Fuck if I know. I thought she was turning the club against us, not literally turning an army. Where the fuck have all these people come from anyway?"

Princess WitchHound stiffens beside me. "This is going to take some serious explanation with the Court and coven. How have we missed all these dead bodies?"

I can hear Nyx giggling away, clearly enjoying this scene and our ignorance. "Fools. You didn't think I only stayed in this town, did you? What fun would that have been?"

I shake my head. Of course. That's why I couldn't feel her soul in the vicinity. The other souls in the town were masking hers. She wasn't around but they were—there's only so many I can answer at the same time.

Bollocks, she played me way too good. Death's gonna have my arse for this.

"Melaina, you're on Thalia. Savage, Crusher, you're on the baby brats. Princess, you're with me. I'm gonna need that power of yours."

Without another word, we disperse into the foray, wild screams and the sounds of ripping flesh bathing the night air. Nyx backs up, seeing me coming for her. I look to Princess. "You got something to hold her still in that arsenal of yours? Anything that blocks her from running away?"

She nods once, and I see the fissures of magic spark between her hands like bolts of electricity. Nyx panics, head turning from side to side, and she figures out which route to take. Clearly, she hadn't made the time to take note of the creatures that already lived here. This is her rookie mistake.

I let my wings out, getting ready to pin the bitch back in the Infernum for good.

"Now!" Princess calls out. I see a momentary blip in energy that flattens Nyx to the earth, almost as though she is paralyzed. I don't waste time.

I scoop the vampire-demon up, chaining her body to mine. Above us a portal opens before I even have time to summon one, and I see Princess manipulating the elements for me. I give her a nod, and disappear as Nyx and I are sucked into the vacuum, tossed and turned and spat back out into her place of torment.

She slams her body into me over and over as she tries to escape the bindings wrapped around her.

"It's over, Nyx. I told you this is where you're meant to be." I untether myself from her and offer the Infernum walls her arms. It reaches out and pulls her in, sucking her into the framework, until only her face is visible.

"What are you doing to me?" she screams, utter fear cloaking her face.

I shake my head. "This is your own doing. The Infernum's reacting to the punishment level you deserve. I warned you, you were making it much worse for yourself. So long, bitch! I look forward to seeing you in the next millennium!"

I zap back out of the place, only to have my being pushed and pulled in a new direction. I thump onto hard rock—red, fiery, noisy Hell replaced with dark, quiet, and somber.

"Well, you're not such a fuckup after all, Shade."

I stand, taking a second to get my bearings. There's nothing like a good brain shake to get you all confused.

"Do I get a raise?" I joke, enjoying Death's cheerier side. He's even wearing a bright blue suit. Guess I did something right for a change.

"I thought you would've asked for something much different. Something to do with a certain supernatural town."

I quirk an eyebrow, wondering what he's getting at. "What would I want with that place?"

Death chuckles. It's a throaty laugh I've not heard before. I wonder how often he does it. "You can't fool me, Shade. I made you, and that town gave you a glimpse of a different life. One with a certain nymph-like damsel."

I try not to blush, but even in this skelly form, it's a little difficult not to when your creator, otherwise known as Dad, starts talking to you about the motions of human interaction. "It would've been nice to see where that life could've taken me. But it's not for me. We both know that."

Death shrugs as though it doesn't matter. "You'll always have the ability to go back there. Especially with that tattoo imprinted on your arm. That'll never change. See you around, Shade."

I'm falling, the ground disappearing, and I'm popping back out of a portal.

"Well, that was weird," I comment to myself, noting the ground I've landed on. What did Death mean?

"Oh, so you're not just fucking off then? I thought you'd gone back to that cold heartedness I first met. You can thank me now."

I smile at Melaina, at the hard time she's giving me. I knew it. I've won her over. Back in the cemetery, I'm surrounded by the bodies of

Nyx's victims, and on their feet are Savage, Crusher, Princess WitchHound, and most important of all, Thalia.

I walk up to her, reaching for her hands, which she's already presenting me. "I'm so sorry. Are you all right? Did she hurt you?"

Thalia shakes her head, tears welling up in her eyes. "I'm okay." Her throat catches on a sob, and it makes me mad to see her so sad. This is all my doing.

"You're safe now, I promise."

She lunges at me, throwing her arms around my neck, burying her head in my chest. I don't know how to react; she's surprised me. Is she finally accepting me? I fold my arms around her tiny waist, pulling her in tight. Over her shoulder, I see Melaina motion to the guys to scramble out of there, but Princess stops her from giving me this moment of bliss. I don't blame her. This night is barely over.

"We've got quite the mess to clean up, which you're definitely sticking around for, reaper. And you can answer to the Court. I'm not taking the fall for this."

I shake my head, a smile gracing my face. "I didn't expect you to. I'm looking forward to finally meeting this Court you keep threatening me with. But first I have one more important matter to attend to."

"Oh no, you—" Princess begins, but luckily Melaina covers her mouth, stopping the little witch from her tirade.

I look at Thalia, her beautiful blue eyes beaming up at me like I've suddenly become her white knight. It's not an attribute I even deserve, not after everything I've put her through. But it's this look in her eyes that makes me selfish enough to ask the unthinkable.

"Thalia, I know I've made a lot of mistakes. And I know I've got a lot to learn. Hell, I don't even know what's going on anymore—Death left me with quite the mixed message. But there's one thing I know for certain, and I don't want to fuck it up any more than I have done."

"Oh, just spit it out already, Shade!" Melaina yells, and I can imagine her rolling her eyes behind my back.

"Thalia, will you help me do this the right way and let me take you out on a date?"

"Finally!" I hear Melaina call in the background, but I'm too hung up on the beauty in front of me to give it much attention. Thalia stares, searching my face, for what I don't know. The silence stretches on forever, and I don't know what to make of it.

Fuck me, I've pushed too far. Took her outreach and pressed too hard. Fuck it. Fuck.

She reaches up on tiptoes and presses a quick kiss to my cheek.

Oh, crap. Here comes the disappointment. Okay, I can do this. I can act graciously. Don't be a big baby.

"Yes, Shade. I would love that."

FUCK YEAH!

EPILOGUE

HORIZONS

THREE MONTHS LATER

"Shade, I'm ready."

I glance up from the newspaper I've been reading and see Thalia standing in nothing but bright pink lacy lingerie that grips onto her curves. I'm instantly hard and having to adjust myself for a more comfortable position on the seat.

"You are beautiful." I can't take my eyes off her. I'm sure they're bulging out of their sockets like I'm a cartoon character. "You can't wear that at the club tonight." The thought of another man enjoying this view right now kills me.

She saunters over to me, straddling my lap, her core teasingly placed over my cock. "I'm not working tonight," she whispers in my ear, teeth grazing my lobe and down my neck. "I'm ready for you."

She kisses me hard, moaning deeply as our tongues fuse together. It's like fireworks of passion exploding in my mind.

"Are you sure?" I gently pull her away, checking her eyes for honesty.

"Never been more positive in my life. I trust you, Shade."

I scoop her up in my arms and carry her to the bedroom, knocking over vases in my haste. I lose myself in her lips again as I lay her on the bed, hovering over her curvaceous body. I have to control my excitement, or I'll be ejaculating before I even enter her.

"Make love to me."

I'm lost in her doe eyes as she rips my clothing to pieces and leaves them to scatter on the floor. It's here I see she's been holding back on me, as she gets on top, losing the seductive underwear she used to lure me here.

She kisses me wildly, eyes feral with lust, and lowers herself onto my cock, her pussy taking all of me in. She moans wildly, and I'm surrounded in pleasure as she rocks back and forth, my cock slipping in and out of her, each time filling her up even more.

I have to squeeze my bloody toes to keep from coming already. I flip her onto her back, leaving kisses from her neck to her navel. I flick my tongue over her clit and listen to her moan, hips bucking against my face.

She's so fucking sexy.

I slip a finger inside her, setting a slow rhythm as I circle my tongue on her swollen clit. She pants loudly, hips matching my movements.

She reaches for my head, tugging me upward until we're face to face.

"Together," she says, and I need no extra explanation from her. She wants our first orgasm together, as though it means something more.

I take her lips again, greedy for every sensation she gives me, and I feel her impatience clawing at me as she flattens me on my back again. My girl likes to take control.

She slams her pussy onto my cock and rides me hard, giving me zero time to savor the pleasure. There's no mercy here.

I suck her left nipple whilst rubbing the right, and she pounds harder, clenching my shaft tightly. "That's it, baby. You feel so fucking good."

She bites her lip as she swirls her hips, and I struggle to contain myself.

I lick my thumb and reach for her clit, watching her head tilt back with pleasure as she moans louder. It turns me on as she calls my name, reaching toward an orgasm.

"Oh, Shade. I'm gonna, I'm gonna . . ." She cries out. I feel her pussy tightening even more, and it sends me over the edge, shooting my cum deep inside her whilst hers drips down my balls.

She collapses on top of me, her heavy breathing in synchronization with mine. I kiss her tenderly, savoring the moment.

"Don't crash on me yet, Shade. The night's only just begun."

I smile, hopeful with the promise. "I love you, Thalia."

She pauses, eyes wide as though I've shocked her. I begin to retract, not wanting to ruin this perfect moment now that she's completely let me in.

She smiles. "Got ya!" She giggles. "I love you too, Shade."

We hope you enjoyed this story in the Havenwood Falls series featuring a variety of supernatural creatures. The series is a collaborative effort by multiple authors.

Books in the Havenwood Falls Sin & Silk series:

Taming the Beast by Nadirah Foxx
Plans Laid Bare by JD Nelson
Shift of Fate by Victoria Escobar
Stolen Wishes by Victoria Flynn
Damned Allure by Justine Winter
Savage Salvation by Kristie Cook
Dark Seduction by Michele G. Miller & R.K. Ryals
Soul Laid Bare by JD Nelson
Stray With Me by E.J. Fechenda
Chase the Flames by Desiree Lafawn
Flirting With Death by Nadirah Foxx

Also try the signature line, Havenwood Falls, the historical paranormal line, Legends of Havenwood Falls, and stories from the local supernatural college in Sun & Moon Academy.

Stay up to date at www.HavenwoodFalls.com

Subscribe to our reader group and receive free stories and more!

ABOUT THE AUTHOR

Justine Winter is the author of the bestselling paranormal romance series Nature's Destiny. She is the proud owner of an MA degree in Creative Writing, and currently divides her time between living in South West Wales and London. Justine loves food, hates coffee, and gobbles up books like they're oxygen. She's often geeky, always funny, and claims her dad jokes will go down in history.

You can stay up to date and in touch with her pretty much on all social media platforms; she's everywhere!

Sign up to her newsletter
   Facebook
   Twitter
   Instagram

ACKNOWLEDGMENTS

Firstly, I'd like to thank Kristie for creating the Havenwood Falls world and opening it up for other authors to collaborate. I am honored to be involved in this amazing universe. I had such fun creating Shade the reaper. He's almost a paranormal version of my character Grayson in Wicked Sunshine. They share a likeness for humor and banter. And both guys have exceptional taste in women.

Thank you to the authors whose characters I've used to help push Shade along in his quest—I couldn't have done it without them.

A big thanks to my readers; I hope I brought you some laughter and that you enjoyed this book. Thank you for your support.

Now I'm heading back to the Winterverse: there's lots of writing to be done in the Winter Cave.

Speak soon, Wolves.
Alpha J - XO

AN EXCERPT

~ A Havenwood Falls Sin & Silk Novella ~

HAVENWOOD FALLS

Sin & Silk

Savage Salvation

KRISTIE COOK

Savage Salvation (A Havenwood Falls Sin & Silk Novella) by Kristie Cook

I never understood the draw of the biker scene. In fact, knowing what I did, I hated it. But Pops swore if anyone could keep me protected, it was the Swords of the Infernal Night in New Orleans. A band of supernatural criminals who think women are possessions, if you ask me. And they haven't kept us safe. Pops is dead, but his murderers are after me, all because my inner kelpie became the first in generations to grow a horn. My name is Reyna Moreno, and yep, I'm a damn unicorn. Which makes me more valuable than the Hope Diamond.

To keep me protected, my brother hauls me off to some gods-forsaken town in Colorado where another SIN chapter "takes us in." Takes me prisoner is more like it. It wouldn't be so bad if my sexy-as-hell warden wasn't such an ass. And wasn't only a biker, but one of the MC's leaders.

He looks at me like he wants to own me. I'm not one to be owned. He's not one to be denied.

They call him Savage for a reason. He's a hellhound and a savage beast. And he would be my undoing . . . but maybe I could be his salvation.

SAVAGE SALVATION

BY KRISTIE COOK

The service came to a close, and everyone stood, the metal chairs creaking almost as loudly as all the leather in the room. I stared at the focal point of the space—the gleaming wooden box dressed in flowers flowing over its edges—as several pairs of heavy boots thudded toward it. At the direction of some guy I'd spoken with only briefly, the six men gathered around the box and lifted.

I stood, turned, and hurried down the aisle, out the other way, my heels clicking in loud echoes on the tile floor as I crossed the lobby. The door nearly knocked over a group of girls when I threw it open, and they yelped as they jumped out of the way. They bitched and moaned, straightening their skin-tight dresses that barely covered the goods. The skanks had no respect. This was a funeral, for mother's sake, and they were dressed like they were auditioning for their next role in a porn.

"Rey." The deep, familiar voice called after me, but I ignored him, heading for my car. I slid into the two-seater Benz, but didn't quite get the door closed before Niall grabbed it. "Reyna. Don' be like this." His Scottish accent came thickly when he was mad.

"Go to hell."

"C'mon, sis."

My jaw clenched. "Don't call me that. You're not my brother."

"For all intents and purposes—"

"What do you want?" I pressed the Start button, and the engine purred to life.

"You're coming to the cemetery, right?"

"Of course I am," I muttered.

My gaze stayed forward, but in my periphery, I saw his thick beard bob as he nodded, then he closed the door. I inhaled deeply and blew the air out slowly, refusing to shed a tear. Unable to, if I was honest. I hadn't yet been able to cry for the man who'd been like an uncle to me, who'd taken a sort of fatherly role when my own had passed. After another deep breath, I followed the procession to the cemetery, also known as the city of the dead. The above-ground tombs and mausoleums lined the pathways like buildings lined the city streets.

Pops didn't get a traditional New Orleans funeral. No jazz music and parading through the streets. Besides all the other reasons, the club wouldn't allow it. Like they should have any say. The New Orleans chapter of the Swords of the Infernal Night motorcycle club, SIN or SIN-NO for short, shouldn't have a say at all in our lives, as far as I was concerned. In fact, if it were up to me, this would be the last time I'd see any of them. Pops trusted them all with our lives, and he lost his for it. I would never trust any of them again.

Not that I ever did in the first place.

I liked to think Niall, who had been like a brother to me, looked out for us, but the rest of them? To hell with them all. They didn't do their job.

I went for a drive once I made sure Pops was in his final resting place, two Harleys rumbling loudly behind me the whole time. Supposedly the two members of SIN were there to guard me, but I couldn't fathom what they thought they could do from back there if I were attacked. It wasn't like the people after me could be taken down with a bullet. If that were the case, Pops would still be alive.

My phone rang, and I ignored it. It persisted until I finally hit the answer button on the steering wheel.

"Reyna," Niall's Scottish lilt came over the car speakers. "Come on home, lass."

"That's not my home." I hadn't been to my home in months.

"Well then, come to *my* home."

"Why? So you can make me a prisoner?"

"We need to talk. Plans have been made."

"Screw you and your plans, Niall. Look where it got us. Pops is—" I hiccupped before continuing— "dead, and I—"

"You're goin' to be okay. It's been arranged. Just come to the club house. You know I hate talking on these things. Especially about this."

He had a point there. We were practically screaming "here I am" at all those who wanted to find me.

"Don't make us force you," he added.

I blew out a sigh. "Fine. I'm on my way. But one thing, Niall."

"What?"

"I'm nobody's bitch. Not yours. Not anyone's. And I'm certainly not an old lady or anybody's property. So stop treating me like I am."

"I'm not. I'm treating you with concern for your safety, which is my job, my qu—"

"Don't you fucking say it." I disconnected the call before he said the word that made me want to hurl every time I heard it. Gah! A shudder ran through me. I'd rather he call me sis or anything else than the word he'd been about to say.

The two bikers followed me like puppy dogs through the streets into an industrial area a few blocks from the French Quarter. As soon as I turned in to the driveway, the gate across it started rolling to the side, and I pulled in. The compound was lit up in more ways than one. The club was obviously having some kind of celebration of life ceremony—just another excuse for everyone to drink until they passed out. I knew this was supposed to be a big honor, since Pops had been a friend of the club but never an actual member, but it felt like salt followed by tequila in my wounds. And not in the good way. Drunk members, friends of the club, hangers-on, and groupies whooped and hollered from inside the brightly lit main building, and the moans and grunts of people fornicating were scattered across the grounds outside. It had only just grown dark. It was going to be a long night.

Niall opened my door for me before I even cut the engine. He stood there in loose jeans, motorcycle boots, a black T-shirt, and his leather vest, called a cut in MC terms, covered in patches. One of them said "Torq," his road name—what everyone here called him. He angled his dark head toward a smaller building to the right of the main one before turning, the large patch of a skull with its head impaled by a rose-wrapped sword staring back at me.

I followed silently, surprised to be heading toward the small structure. The big house was where some of the members lived and where Pops and I had been staying the last several months. It also housed the party area, with a long bar, a couple of pool tables, and a few threadbare couches stained with substances I didn't want to think too hard about or I'd need to bleach my brain. It stunk, pun intended, having supernatural senses when you lived where there was practically an orgy every other night. This small building, though, served as the club's church—where they held their meetings and did their business.

I didn't like the idea of being a piece of their business, but at least they had the decency to invite me in on the subject this time around. Well, not really invite. It'd still been more like an order, even if it had been delivered by my so-called brother. And I was only assuming that was what was going on—that this was about me. Pops may have been a friend of the club, but I'd never been all that friendly with them. In fact, I'd always made my disdain quite clear. And now Pops was dead, and they needed to figure out what to do with me. Throwing me out would be disrespectful to Pops's memory. And while I thought of them as no more than criminal scum, I couldn't deny that the club did have a code, and respect was important to them.

And it wasn't just about Pops.

They'd have to deal with kelpies worldwide—some of whom were already in town for the funeral—if the club tried anything stupid with me. Considering the number of kelpies in the various chapters of the club, that'd create a lot of extra tension for the SIN president to deal with. Of course, he was known for doing such things when he was bored, and I was pretty sure he'd grown bored of me a long time ago when I refused to screw him.

"Reyna, come in and have a seat," Prez said when Niall and I entered the building. I paid him little notice, but I could feel his gaze undressing me as he motioned toward a room with a large conference table surrounded by a dozen or more chairs. The dim lighting from a table lamp in the corner created shadows, the far end of the room doused in obsidian darkness—but I could sense the people there. Or beings, anyway. As I entered, a hint of sulfur burned my nose, but then it was followed by a scent that was musky, warm, and mouth-watering, making my belly tighten and my thighs squeeze together. *What the hell?* Whoever was back there, they definitely weren't human and not kelpie, either—not my kind here to protect me.

Not that my people were a huge threat to most of the SIN members in any chapter, including those here. They were all supernaturals, many of whom were a lot more badass than people who shifted into horses. Unless there was a body of water around and the other supe couldn't swim, kelpies were mostly dangerous only to humans.

Except me.

I was the first in many generations of our kind to grow a horn. One single horn, right out of the top of my forehead. Yep, I was a damn unicorn. The silver horn had first broken through when I was twelve, only a few months after my first shift. It'd hurt like a bitch, and even in my human form, I still had a scar at my hairline, barely visible under all my curls. I'd only been able to shift a few times in the thirteen years since then, because as soon as word got out, my life was endangered. From my horn to my tears to the hairs in my mane and tail, I had way too many valuable parts. Parts that some would love to harvest.

Hunters came for me almost right away, in my home country of Brazil, and killed my parents. Pops, who wasn't really related but had been like an uncle to me, escaped with Niall and me, whisking us off to America. Niall had always been like an adopted brother, coming to us as an orphan when I was nine and he was supposedly fifteen. I didn't learn until we were found again a year ago that he was much, much older—kelpies, like all fae, lived very long lives while retaining youthful appearances, especially when we used glamour—and that he'd been groomed all his life to be a warrior to protect the future queen. He'd been sent to Brazil when a fae Seer prophesized that the next kelpie queen would come from our small South American town. We hadn't known then, before I'd ever even shifted, that this queen was me. Because for some reason in kelpie law, the one with the horn ruled.

I really did not want to rule.

At least, I didn't want to rule a smattering of supernaturals that hadn't been a true herd in generations. The kelpies had escaped to the earthly realm during a devastating war in our Faerie homeland many centuries ago. They stayed together in Scotland for a while, but rifts over time sent more and more away, and after the last unicorn queen died, what remained of the herd scattered. If the need arose, they'd be compelled to come together once again for me, but could they ever be a herd again? Especially since so many had joined a different kind of herd—the SIN MC? Whom would they truly be loyal to if it came down to it? Me and each other or their patch?

Hopefully, the need would never arise.

As I walked farther into the room as though drawn to the far end by that delicious smell, annoyance doused the desire when I noticed my designer luggage piled by the doorway. I turned on Niall, Prez, and Chintz, the VP, while trying to tamper my anger—not because they were kicking me out, but because they'd dared to touch my personal property.

"Not wasting any time, I see." I gave them a saccharine smile. "No worries, though. I wasn't planning on staying anyway."

Niall reached out, cupping my elbow and leading me toward a chair. "Sit, Rey."

"I'm not a dog." My patience was waning. Someone at the far end of the room snickered.

Niall sighed. "Sit down and listen. Like I said, we have a plan. It's all taken care of."

None of the bikers sat, so neither did I. "I don't need your plan."

"Ya do," Niall insisted.

"He's right," Prez said, his voice deep and full of promise of dark, ugly things. His beady eyes were barely visible behind all his dark facial hair, but I felt them on me, the sensation like cold slime. He crossed his log-thick arms over his barrel chest. "The hunters know you're here this very second. Our guys followed two of them who were following you."

"They're dead," Chintz said flatly. He leaned his thin yet sinewy arms on the back of one of the chairs, also appraising me as I let that sink in. My insides felt sick, but I refused to squirm in their presence.

"You're willing to go to war over me, yet you're kicking me out?" I asked.

Chintz shrugged. "We've gone to war for lesser reasons."

"We swore an oath to Pops," Prez said as a better explanation. "We don't go back on our word."

"Yet you're kicking me out," I repeated, my hand gesturing toward my suitcases.

"We're sendin' you to a safe place," Niall said.

Every muscle in my body tensed up. "You're *sending* me to a safe place? What does that mean? You're not sending me anywhere! Who do you think you are?"

"Reyna!" Niall barked, and I'd never heard him say my name so sharply. "You need to listen. It's for your own god damn safety."

My ample chest heaved as I tried to regain control of my anger. My inner beast had awakened. I'd learned long ago how to contain her, but she always showed interest when my emotions rose, hoping I'd finally let her break free. This would be the absolute worst time to indulge her, especially with strangers in the room, so I forced her to settle down and go back to sleep. Crossing my arms over my breasts, I cocked my head, my only indication that I was listening.

"A SIN chapter in Colorado has agreed to provide you protection," Prez said.

My jaw dropped. "*Colorado?* No way in hell!"

"They'll take you in, under the wards of their town," Prez continued gruffly, ignoring my outburst.

"It's a small town in the mountains," Niall added. "I bet you'll love it."

I'll bet I won't.

Someone on the far end emerged from the darkness—over six feet tall, sandy brown hair, wearing sunglasses—at night, inside, in the dark—and a leather cut with a small patch that said Pirate and another under it that said President. That vague hint of sulfur wafted to my nose. Demon, perhaps?

"Our town isn't like anyplace else," he said, his voice deep and raspy. "There's no safer place."

"No offense, Mr. . . ."

"Pirate," he said.

"Mr. Pirate."

"Just. *Pirate*," the stranger growled.

I blinked, suppressing the urge to roll my eyes. "Okay, no offense, *Pirate*, but these assholes here couldn't protect us, so what makes you think you can?"

That snicker sounded again from the dark end of the room.

"And I can't go all the way to Colorado," I hurried on, because my question had been rhetorical and I didn't want them thinking they needed to answer it. "I have a business to run, which these dumb shits seem to have forgotten."

I turned back to Niall and Prez with a raised brow.

No, I didn't want to rule a kingdom. But I did want to rule an empire.

And I'd already been on my way to building it with my plus-size fashion and lifestyle blog and specialty lingerie designs when the hunters discovered our location and we had to go into hiding a year ago. That made running a business a little difficult, and I knew my clients were almost out of patience. Good thing for me that they loved my designs too much to completely give up on me.

But disappearing to a small mountain town in Colorado where they probably didn't even have indoor plumbing, let alone internet service? That would be a career killer.

"Your laptop's packed," Niall said. "All your business stuff is. You've already been running it remotely for a year. You haven't lost any business yet, have you?"

"I haven't gained any, either," I sniped back. My brain knew it wasn't Niall's or anyone else's fault that the hunters were after me. Somewhere deep down I also knew it wasn't his or the MC's fault that I'd been found. But damn it, it was their fault that Pops was dead and we were even having this discussion.

All I wanted was to be in my own bed in my own home, preparing for tomorrow's work day like any normal person. Just like I had been before the hunters had discovered my general location, and now they'd come way too close. If Niall and the MC had done their jobs properly, I could have at least had some semblance of my old life. We definitely wouldn't be discussing some trip to Colorado or the future of my business that wasn't looking so promising anymore. So repressing my anger wasn't easy.

Besides, if I didn't stay angry, the grief would kick in.

"Don' be difficult, Rey," Niall practically begged, his accent thicker than usual. He knew I had a soft spot for it. "Yeh know yeh can't stay here, love. Yeh can't leave this compound and expect to live. And how many people here are you goin' to let die for yeh?"

I scowled. He knew exactly what buttons to push.

"Yer life, yer people's lives, these people's lives—no matter how much yeh don't like 'em—they're more importan' than anythin', aren't they?" he continued, tilting his head as he stared me down with piercing sapphire eyes, challenging me to argue further.

I opened my mouth to do just that, because I was stubborn like that. There had to be another way. No, I wouldn't let anyone here die while protecting me. Niall was the only one who had any kind of place in my heart, but just because I didn't like the MC and their crowd didn't mean I wanted them dead. Especially not for me.

But Colorado couldn't possibly be our only choice.

Those words were on the tip of my tongue when the other figure stepped out of the shadows at the far end of the room, that delicious scent wafting toward me again. And if my body's reaction meant anything, any other options had just been wiped off the table.

Purchase *Savage Salvation* where books are sold.

www.ingramcontent.com/pod-product-compliance
Lightning Source LLC
Chambersburg PA
CBHW052010170626
46808CB00007B/2866